# The Magic Needle

## and

## Other Stories

by
ENID BLYTON

*Illustrated by*
Val Biro

AWARD PUBLICATIONS LIMITED

For further information on Enid Blyton please contact
www.blyton.com

ISBN 1-84135-441-4

First published by Award Publications Limited 2001
This edition first published 2005

Published by Award Publications Limited, The Old Riding
School, Welbeck Estate, Nr Worksop, Notts S80 3LR

Printed in Singapore

# CONTENTS

# The
# Magic Needle

Tricks and Slippy were tailors. They made coats and cloaks for all the little folk in Breezy Village and the other villages round about.

"We don't get paid nearly enough for our work," grumbled Tricks. "We ought to get ever so much more!"

"Yes. If we were paid properly, we should have a nice little motorcar by now to deliver all our goods," said Slippy.

"Oh, you and your motorcar. You're always talking about that," said Tricks. "Now what I want is a lovely little boat to sail on the river."

"Fiddlesticks!" began Slippy, and then he had to stop because a customer had just come in. It was Jinky the brownie. He flung a coat down on the table.

"Look there!" he said. "Bad work again! All the buttons fell off in a day, and this collar has come unstitched. No wonder we don't pay you top prices, you're so careless!"

He stalked out, looking very cross.

"Blow!" said Slippy, picking up the coat. "Now I've got to sew those horrid little buttons on all over again. I wish we had a magic needle, Tricks. That's what we want. But nowadays nobody ever hears of a thing like that."

"A magic needle!" said Tricks, looking up in excitement. "Why – my old granny used to have one. She did, she did! I'd forgotten about it all these years, but now I've suddenly remembered it."

"Goodness! A real magic needle?" said Slippy, amazed. "Where is it?"

"Well – I suppose my old granny has still got it somewhere," said Tricks.

"Go and ask her to lend it to us," said Slippy at once.

"Ooooh, no, I wouldn't dare. She doesn't like me," said Tricks. "She says I'm always up to tricks, and she shouts at

me whenever she sees me, so I never go to see her now."

"What a pity," said Slippy. "Shall I go and see her? She might show me the needle, mightn't she – and oh, Tricks! I've just thought of a most wonderful idea!"

"What?" said Tricks. "I don't really think much of your ideas, you know."

"Listen, I'll go and visit your granny and I'll get her to show me the needle – then I'll take her needle and put one of our needles in its place! See?"

"Yes! Yes, that's quite a good idea," said Tricks, pleased. "I know the size it was – and it had a very big eye, I remember. I believe I've got one that looks just like it!"

He hunted about in his box of needles, and took one out. "Here it is – just like Granny's magic one – except that there's no magic in this one!"

"Does the real magic one sew all by itself?" asked Slippy.

"Oh, yes – it sews and sews and sews. You've only got to place it on top of a

pile of cloth, and say 'Coats' or 'Cloaks', or whatever you want, and the needle sets to work at once, and hey presto, there's a pile of coats sitting there before you know where you are!"

"Does it cut the cloth up, too, before it sews it?" asked Slippy, astonished.

"Not exactly," said Tricks. "It sews the cloth into the right shapes – sleeves and so on – and then all the bits and pieces fall away, the coat turns itself inside out, and there you are!"

"Marvellous! Wonderful!" said Slippy.

"I'd simply love to see that happening."

"Well, you will if you go to see my granny," Tricks said, with a grin. "But be very careful of her when you go, because she's very fond of scolding people."

Slippy set off the very next day with Tricks's needle in a needle-case. He caught the bus and went to Hush-Hush Village. He soon came to the house of Tricks's grandmother, a lovely, neat little place with pretty curtains in all the windows.

The old lady didn't seem very pleased to see him. "Hm!" she said. "So you're a friend of my grandson, are you, Slippy? Slippy by name and Slippy by nature, I wouldn't be at all surprised. What have you come for?"

"Just to see you," said Slippy. "Tricks has said such a lot about you. He said you were such a nice old lady, and so very friendly and kind."

"Hm! Did he tell you I've been kind enough to scold him a hundred times for his bad ways and mischievous tricks?" said the old lady. "Tell him to come and

see me again, because I've got scolding number one-hundred-and-one waiting for him."

Slippy began to think that Tricks's grandmother wasn't a very kind old lady.

"Er – is it true that you once had a magic needle?" he asked, thinking that he had better find out before some kind of scolding came his way.

"Quite true," said the old woman. "Look in the bottom drawer of that chest, in the left-hand corner, and you'll see a pin-cushion. The needle is stuck in it.

Bring it out and I'll show you what it can do."

Slippy found the needle easily. He took it out of the pin-cushion excitedly and gave it to the old woman. She threaded it with red cotton, pulled Slippy's lovely new red hanky out of his pocket and stuck the needle into the corner of it.

"Doll's dress," she said, in a loud voice. And, to Slippy's enormous surprise, that needle set to – and, in no time at all, there was a beautiful little doll's dress lying on the table, all neatly trimmed and finished! The needle had slipped in and out so fast, with a long red thread behind it, that Slippy had found it quite difficult to follow.

"Marvellous!" said Slippy. "But what about my lovely new hanky? You shouldn't have made a doll's dress out of it."

"Don't you talk to me like that," said the old lady, as if she was going to shout at Slippy. "You'll just have to blow your nose on a doll's dress, that's all. And if you dare to . . ."

Slippy fled! He pushed the red doll's dress into his pocket. He was grinning broadly. Aha! He had just had time to exchange the two needles! He had the magic one in his needle-case – and he had left the one he had brought, safely pushed into the pin-cushion!

Tricks was delighted when Slippy showed him the needle. "Well done, Slippy!" he said. "I never thought you'd be able to get it. Granny's eyes are so sharp, I was sure she'd spot you exchanging the needles. Now we'll be able to make some money. Goodness, we'll really be able to make some money! My word, we'll be able to make a dozen coats a day now!"

"I didn't like your granny," said Slippy. "She was rather rude to me. I thought she was going to start shouting at me."

"She probably was," said Tricks. "Well, we will never, never go near her again, so we won't have any more trouble from her. Now – let's go out and buy all kinds of cloth, and get that needle to start working on new coats tonight."

So out they went and spent a lot of money on new cloth. They staggered home with it, and set it on the table.

"Yellow cloth, red cloth, blue, purple, black, green and orange," said Tricks. "My, what a wonderful lot of handsome coats we'll have! Needle, listen to me. Here are reels of cotton to match each cloth. You are a sensible needle, and will take the right cotton from each reel. I will thread you the first time, and after that you will thread yourself, just as you used to do for my granny!"

"Most remarkable," said Slippy, watching him in delight. Tricks threaded the magic needle with red cotton and then stuck it into a pile of red cloth.

"Coats!" he said, and dear me, you should have seen that needle! It flew in and out, in and out, and there were the two sleeves and soon the collar was made, and the lapels, and the coat itself – then the sleeves were sewn in, quick as lightning.

"Buttons! We've forgotten to buy the buttons," said Slippy suddenly, and he rushed out to buy buttons of all colours.

The needle was wonderful with buttons. It sewed them all on in the right places, as quick as a flash and as strongly as could be!

"There's the first coat," said Tricks, pleased. "And look at all the bits and pieces that have fallen off just as if they'd been cut away. Really, this is a very powerful needle."

"It is," said Slippy. "Shall we have our supper and go to bed? I don't really want to watch the needle making coats all night long. It's rather tiring to see something working so hard."

So they had buns and cocoa and went off to bed, leaving the magic needle flying in and out as if it was worked by lightning!

What a marvellous thing!

They fell asleep in their two little beds. The needle went on working by itself in the workroom. In three hours it had finished the pile of coats – sixteen beautifully finished coats lay in a heap, with shiny little buttons down the fronts.

The needle had no more cloth. It took

a look round with its one eye. Ah – what about the tablecloth? It must make a coat out of that. So it did – and a very nice little check coat it was!

Then it took another look round. Ah – what about that hearth-rug? That would make a fine warm coat!

And down swooped the needle and in about ten minutes there was no rug to be seen – but in its place was a very warm little coat, with snippings on the floor around it!

The needle was really enjoying itself tremendously. It made coats out of the curtains. It tried to make one out of a cushion, but it couldn't. It made coats out of the dusters, and tea cloths, and even out of a pair of stockings. Really, it was a remarkably ingenious needle.

Soon there was nothing left downstairs for it to sew. So it flew upstairs, looking round with its one eye. When it saw all the bedclothes on the two beds it was simply delighted!

And very soon it was busy making coats out of all the sheets and blankets on Slippy's bed. But as Slippy was lying fast asleep in them, it made things very difficult for the needle. It had to join all the coats together around Slippy, and in the end the bed looked like an enormous sack with sleeves sticking out of it here, there and everywhere! Slippy couldn't be seen – he was inside somewhere!

He woke up and began to wriggle. Whatever had happened? Where was he? He called out to Tricks. But Tricks was now being sewn up, too, in half a dozen

coats which were made up of his sheets
and blankets, and even one of the corners
of his eiderdown. Oh dear, oh dear!

Slippy and Tricks shouted and
wriggled and they both rolled off their
beds with a bump. What a dreadful night
they had! The needle couldn't quite
understand what had happened and kept
going up to them and pricking them.
That made them yell all the more!

They rolled to the door. They bumped all the way down the little flight of stairs – *bumpity – bumpity-bump-bump*!

But they couldn't undo themselves, because when that needle sewed, it sewed very well indeed!

"Slippy! We'll have to roll out of the door and into the front garden," gasped Tricks at last. "We simply must get help. It's morning now, because I can hear the milkman coming."

He rolled himself hard against the door and it burst open. Out went Slippy and Tricks, looking most peculiar all sewn up in sheets and blankets, with long sleeves flapping about all over the place!

The milkman was amazed. He dropped his milk-can and stood there, staring.

"Help! Help!" he shouted. "There's something very strange going on here!"

Well, very soon the neighbours came out and found out just what had happened. Tricks told them about the antics of the magic needle, and begged his friends to snip the stitches and let him out.

At last he was freed from the mass of sheet-and-blanket coats, and stood up, blinking in the sunlight. And, oh dear – when he saw his curtains and rug and tablecloth and everything else made into coats, he wept loudly. So did Slippy.

"The needle's still busy!" cried Slippy, suddenly. "Look, it's got into our chest of drawers and it's making coats out of our vests and pants and trousers and everything!"

"We'll have to take it back to my granny," said Tricks, tears streaming down his face. "Come on. It's no good, that needle will go on and on till it's taken back. We'll be ruined!"

So they had to take the needle back. How they hoped the old lady would be out. But she wasn't! She was watching for them. She knew that Slippy had exchanged the needles – her eyes were just as sharp as the eye of that needle!

Well, you can guess what happened, and why Slippy and Tricks went home howling, and looked sorry for themselves for a whole week. Nobody would buy the coats the needle had made – they said they were afraid of magic coats. So it didn't do them much good to play a silly trick like that on Tricks's grandmother – in fact, they are still trying to undo the stitches in the curtain-coats, and rug-coat and tablecloth-coat, to get them back again.

That needle has taught them not to be lazy, anyhow!

# The Tale of
# the Tadpoles

There was once a small boy called Timmy.
He went fishing one day in a little pond
where some frogs had laid their eggs.
They had laid them in jelly, but now, in
the warm sunshine, the jelly had melted,
and the eggs had hatched out into tiny
little black tadpoles.

How they wriggled and raced round
the pond! They were strange little things,
all tail and head. Timmy wondered what
they were. He put some in a jar and took
them home, with some pondweed for
them to cling to if they wanted to.

"Look, Mum!" he said. "What are these? Haven't I got a lot of the little black wrigglers?"

"Yes, you have. Far too many," said his mother. "Now, Timmy, you like frogs, don't you? Well, these tiny wrigglers will all change into frogs, if you take care of them properly. It will be like magic."

"Gracious! I'd like to watch them turning into frogs," said Timmy, who couldn't imagine how they did it. "But have I really got too many, Mum? I'd like a lot of frogs, you know."

"Well, if you do what most children do, and keep dozens in a small jar, they will all die, for there will not be enough air in the water for them all to breathe," said his mother. "Take all but five or six of them back to the pond, Timmy, and just keep those few."

So Timmy kept five in his jam-jar, and watched them carefully. His mother showed him how to tie a tiny bit of food on a thread and hang it in the jar for them to nibble at. Then he pulled it out again so that it would not go bad, and make the water smelly and cloudy. He left the pondweed in because the tadpoles loved that.

One day he put them out in the jar in the sun. The hot sun warmed the water, and soon the tadpoles rose to the top, turned over and looked as if they were dying. Timmy rushed to his mother at once.

"Oh, Timmy! They're slowly cooking in the sun, poor things!" said his mother, whipping them away to a cool corner, and putting a little cold water into the jar. "Poor creatures! I hope they won't die. Hundreds of poor little tadpoles are cooked every year because children put them into the hot sun!"

"I didn't think," said Timmy, sadly. "I do hope they'll be all right, Mum. I do like them so very much."

They didn't die. They got better when

they felt cool. So Timmy was able to watch the magic that turned the tadpoles, all heads and tails, into tiny frogs with four legs and a little squat body! Their back legs grew, and then their front legs. Their tails became short. Timmy watched them each day, so he knew. He gave them a cork to climb on, when they became tiny frogs, for now they liked to breathe the air.

Then he put them into his garden so that they could find new homes for themselves.

"Eat the grubs and flies for me," he said. "I've been a friend to you – now you can be a friend to me!"

Would you like to see frog magic too? Well, do as Timmy did, then, and keep a few tadpoles in a jar.

# A Bunny
# Family

Once upon a time there was a mother bunny who had four small bunnies in a secret hole. She did not even let the father bunny into this hole at first. She lay there keeping her tiny bunnies warm and cosy. It was a good hole, and it was lined with dry grass and some fur from the mother bunny's own body.

At first the tiny rabbits looked very ugly and strange – for they had no fur, and their eyes were closed. But very soon they grew soft, grey-brown fur, just like their mother's, and when they were twelve days old, they opened their eyes. Mother Bunny was pleased.

"Now you will soon be able to go out with me," she said to her little ones. "The world outside is very good. There is plenty of sweet grass to eat, and the sun is warm and pleasant."

"Can't we go with you now?" said Floppy, the biggest one. His mother said no, they were much too small.

When they were three weeks old, Mother Bunny said they might go out of the hole on their first great adventure. The little bunnies were most excited. Usually, when their mother ran up to the sunshine, she closed up their hole tightly, so that no enemy could get in – and neither could the wee bunnies creep out! But this time she did not stop up the hole. She left it open so that they could all follow her!

They all scrambled out. She led them up a dark tunnel, and then round a bend and into another burrow. The tiny rabbits followed her carefully. They could just see her white bobtail in the darkness. "Are you all there?" she called. "Floppy? Bobtail? Scutter? Downy?"

"Yes, we are here, Mother!" they called back. Then the burrow they were running along seemed to get lighter and lighter – and suddenly all the rabbits were out in the evening sunshine!

The babies blinked their eyes, half frightened, for they had lived in the darkness up till now. They did not understand this bright light – the green grass, the noise of singing birds, and the sight of so many other rabbits!

"So these are our little ones!" said a big rabbit, running up to the little family. "Well, they look a nice little lot! I hope they are good."

"Bunnies, this is your father," said Mother Bunny. "He will teach you many things. Listen to him very carefully."

"The first thing to learn," said the big father rabbit, "is what to do when I make

this noise." He suddenly drummed on the ground with his big hind feet. The little rabbits were startled.

"Now that noise," said their father, "is to tell you that danger is near – a fox, perhaps, who will eat you – and as soon as you hear that noise you must look round for your mother. You will see her running towards your hole, her white tail bobbing up and down. Follow her tail and you will be safe, for she will take you deep into a burrow."

"Yes, Father," said the little rabbits. They ran off to play – and what a fine time they had! They nibbled the grass, as their mother did. They ate a piece of carrot that had been brought from a field by their father. They scampered about in the greatest delight. Then suddenly they heard the drumming noise on the ground: *R-r-r-r-r-r-r*!

They looked round in fright.

"Fox! Fox!" called an older rabbit. The little ones saw their mother running away and they ran after her, watching her bobbing white tail as she ran. They

followed her down a hole – and they were safe!

"You are good, obedient children," said their mother. "Now, it is time for you to rest. Come close to me, all of you, and sleep."

The tired little rabbits cuddled up to their big, furry mother and fell asleep. How happy they were!

The next evening their mother took them out again, and this time she showed them how to dig and scrape away at the earth with their blunt claws.

"You may want to dig a burrow for yourselves one day," she said. "Do it like this – and like this."

They all did as they were told. Then off they went to play once more. They chased the other little rabbits, they popped up and down holes, they learned their way about the dark, winding burrows, and they always kept their ears open for the drumming noise. As soon as they heard that they shot into their holes like lightning! No fox ever caught Floppy, Downy, Bobtail or Scutter!

They are big rabbits now, fat and furry. How do I know? Well, I see them on the hillside each evening as I go by. You can find them there yourselves if you look!

# Here Comes the Wizard!

Once there was a wizard who used to live in a cave on High-Up Hill. But that was a very long time ago, so long that not one of the brownies who went up and down the hill could remember him.

But whenever they came back from the market one or other always said the same thing, "It's a good thing the Wizard of Woolamalooloo is gone. We've bought so many things at the market that he would have a good haul if he popped out of his cave and stopped us."

Then they would all laugh, because nobody lived in the cave now, certainly not a wizard.

The path to the market lay up the hill and down, and passed near the old cave. The brownies loved going to market each

Friday, and coming back with all the things they had bought for their wives and children.

One day a new brownie came to live in Whispering Wood with the others. His name was Smarty, and he certainly was smart. He got better bargains at the market than anyone else.

When he heard the story of the old wizard who once lived in the cave, he thought about it. The next time the brownies walked down the hill near the cave, bringing home their goods from the market, Smarty listened to hear the usual remark. It came!

"It's a good thing the Wizard of Woolamalooloo is gone. We've bought so many things at the market that he would have a good haul if he popped out of his cave and stopped us."

Then Smarty spoke in a very solemn voice. "The Wizard of Woolamalooloo has come to live not far from here. I knew him before I came – a most unpleasant fellow. And he told me that one day he might come back here, hide in his cave

and pop out at us when we were coming back from market."

Everyone looked most alarmed. "I don't believe it," said Stouty, a burly, good-natured little brownie.

"Ho!" said Smarty, "you don't? Well, all I can say is this – that if ever any one of us yells out that he can see the wizard waiting for us, we'd better drop our goods and run down the hill for all we're worth."

"Stuff and nonsense!" said Stouty.

"I don't know," said little Peeko. "If

the old wizard is about, and comes here, I think Smarty's idea is a good one. If we try to run away carrying our heavy goods, we'd soon be caught. Far better to drop our things and go!"

"Well spoken," said Smarty. "Well, I've warned you. We'll all keep watch the very next time, in case the wizard is around! I've a feeling he may be!"

Stouty looked at Smarty, and thought a lot. That wizard wouldn't come! Smarty was making it all up for some reason or other. What was the reason? Stouty thought he could guess!

Now, on the next market day, all the brownies except Stouty went to market as usual, and back again. Smarty went, too, of course. They came back up the hill, and then went down the other side, keeping a sharp lookout for the wizard.

And suddenly Smarty's voice rang out loudly:

"There he is! Behind those trees! I can see him lying in wait for us. Drop your things and run, brownies, run as fast as you can, run, RUN!"

The brownies shrieked and yelled. They dropped all the goods they had bought and ran down the hill at top speed.

All but Smarty. He waited till they were out of sight, then he laughed. He began to pick up the dropped goods, and stuff them into a big sack.

"How foolish they are!" he said. "They

rush off and leave all their goods for me – and there isn't a wizard for miles around."

Then a deep voice spoke from the nearby cave and he nearly jumped out of his skin.

"Smarty! Come here! Bring those goods to me!"

Smarty went pale and jumped. Who was that? "Who are you?" he stammered.

"Well, you told the others," said the voice. "Who used to live here, Smarty? Why, the Wizard of Woolamalooloo. Bring those goods to me, Smarty – and all your own goods, too!"

Smarty wailed in fright. Oh, oh, to think the real wizard was there, after all! What a piece of bad luck. Shaking with fright, he took everything to the cave, and threw it down outside. He could not see inside because it was far too dark.

"Leave the goods there," said the deep voice. "And come inside, Smarty. Come inside and see what happens to nasty little brownies like you. Come inside, Smarty."

But Smarty didn't. He fled over the hill, back to the market, through the town there, and out to the land of Far-Off-and-Forgotten. Never would he go back to Whispering Wood again!

The wizard in the cave chuckled as he saw Smarty tearing away. He came out – and dear me, what was this? He was no wizard! He was just Stouty the brownie, not even dressed up! He picked up the sacks of goods and went down the hill to the town, laughing loudly.

The other brownies gathered round him eagerly:

"Stouty – how did you get our goods?"

"Oh, Stouty, did you see the wizard?"

"Stouty, weren't you afraid?"

"No," said Stouty, with another laugh. "Why, that wizard lost all of his magic powers one day and had to go to work for my great-granny – and he's there still, digging her garden and weeding and watering for her all day long. The Wizard of Woolamalooloo indeed! We all call him Wooly for short and he really wouldn't hurt a fly!"

"You're better than any wizard, Stouty!" said his friends. "We guess Smarty won't come back here any more!"

He won't. He's much too afraid of the wizard who wasn't there!

# Goldie, the Cat Who Said Thank You

"Jean!" called Mother. "I want you to go on an errand for me!"

"Where to?" asked Jean, running up.

"To Mrs Hunt at Home Farm," said her mother. "Fetch me six new-laid eggs, darling. The doctor says Daddy must have lots of them to make him better."

"All right," said Jean, and fetched her little egg basket. "I won't be long, Mummy."

Off she went, over the fields and across the little brown stream to Home Farm.

Mrs Hunt was feeding her chickens when Jean got to the farm. She smiled at the little girl.

"Good morning, my dear," she said. "Does your mother want some of my nice eggs?"

"Yes, we would like six eggs, please," answered Jean. "Where's Philip?"

"Philip's round at the big barn," said Mrs Hunt. "He's got some fine kittens there, if you'd like to see them!"

"Yes, I would!" said Jean. "I'll go now." She ran round to the big barn and went in. There she saw Philip, Mrs Hunt's son, bending over a litter of kittens lying in some hay.

"Hello, Jean!" he said. "Come and look at these! Two of them are real beauties!"

Jean bent over the kittens. Tibs, the mother cat, washed herself calmly and took no notice – she knew Philip and Jean would do no harm.

"They haven't got their eyes open yet," said Philip. "Aren't these two sweet? Their hair is long and silky already. They ought to be fine cats."

"But why don't you like the little third one?" asked Jean. "He looks quite a dear."

"What! That ugly little sandy fellow!" said Philip scornfully. "He's not worth keeping!"

"But he can't help being that colour!" said Jean. "What are you going to do with him?"

"I'll have to drown him," answered Philip. "Mum will only let me keep two."

"Oh, poor wee thing!" cried Jean. "What a shame, just because he's not got long silky hair, like the others! Please don't drown him, Philip!"

"Well, you have him, then," said Philip. "You haven't got a cat, have you?"

"No, I haven't. Oh, I wonder if Mummy would let me have him!" cried Jean, jumping up. "I'll go and ask her about it this very minute!"

She ran to Mrs Hunt and took the eggs. Then, going as fast as she dared, for she was afraid of breaking the precious eggs, she hurried home again.

"Mummy!" she called. "Here are the eggs. And oh, Mummy! Philip's got three kittens, and he's only allowed to keep two. The other will be drowned if I don't have it! Can I have it, Mummy? Oh, please can I?"

"Oh, Jean dear!" said her mother. "I really don't think you can! I simply haven't any money at all to spare to pay for cat food! Since Daddy's been ill, I haven't known how to manage!"

"How much does cat food cost?" asked Jean. "Could I have the kitten if I give you the money that Great-Aunt Jane gives me every Saturday for running her errands for her?"

Mother looked at Jean and thought for a moment.

"Do you want that kitten very badly?" she asked, smiling. "Is it worth that much to you?"

"Oh yes!" answered Jean. "Don't let it be drowned, Mummy, please!"

"Well, you may have it," said her mother. "You can pay me half of your money every Saturday, and keep the rest yourself."

"You darling!" squeaked Jean, and hugged her mother as hard as ever she could. "Thank you."

"Well, you can go and tell Philip," said Mother. "And you can fetch the kitten when it's old enough to leave its mother."

Jean ran off, feeling most excited, and told Philip what she was going to do.

"All right," he said. "It's a good thing for that kitten you came along when you did! I hope that it will be a grateful kitten and will say thank you!"

"Don't be silly, Philip," said Jean. "Cats don't know how to say thank you."

In a few weeks Jean fetched the kitten to her own home. It was a little tabby, thin and not very pretty, but Jean didn't mind about that at all.

"You're certainly worth half my money each week," she said, hugging the kitten to her. "And I'm going to buy a lovely red collar for you."

The kitten loved Jean. It followed her about all over the place, and purred whenever it saw her. It played all sorts of tricks on her, and jumped at her feet as if they were a couple of scampering mice.

Jean loved the kitten, and when the little boy next door laughed at it, and called it "an ugly, common little tabby," she told him he was horrid.

"You shouldn't say that in front of the

kitty," she scolded. "It will make him miserable!"

"Fiddlesticks! Kittens haven't any sense, as everyone knows!" said the boy, laughing.

"This one has!" said Jean, and took her kitten indoors without saying another word.

She couldn't think what to call him at first. Then, because he had fine golden whiskers, she called him Goldie.

He seemed to like his name very much, and always came scampering to Jean when she called him, wherever he happened to be.

"He's not at all a bad little kitten,"

said Mother one day. "He's growing a lovely strong, smooth coat, Jean. He may be quite a nice cat, after all!"

"Of course he will!" said Jean. "I believe he will be beautiful, Mummy!"

"Oh, no dear, not beautiful," said Mother. "He's only just a very ordinary tabby, you know!"

One day Great-Aunt Jane asked Jean what she did with the money she got every week for running her errands on Saturday.

"I give Mummy half of it to help pay for Goldie's food," said Jean. "The rest I spend on all sorts of things."

"Who's Goldie?" asked Great-Aunt Jane.

"He's my own cat," said Jean. "He's a perfect darling."

She told Great-Aunt Jane all about how she came to have him.

"Dear me! That's very interesting!" said Great-Aunt Jane. "I'm very fond of cats. I used to keep some beauties. You must bring your Goldie and let me see him next Saturday."

"Perhaps you won't think he's very beautiful," said Jean. "Nobody seems to think much of him, except me."

"Well, bring him, and I'll tell you exactly what I think," said Great-Aunt Jane with a smile.

So the next Saturday Jean carried Goldie all the way to Great-Aunt Jane's. He had grown into a big cat, and his tail was very long. His eyes were amber green, and his whiskers were still very

golden. He was heavy, but Jean didn't dare to put him down, just in case he ran away and got lost.

"Good morning, Aunt Jane," she panted, when she reached her great-aunt's house at last. "I'm sorry I'm late, but Goldie was so heavy."

"So that's Goldie, is it?" said Great-Aunt Jane, taking him from Jean. She stroked him and he purred loudly. Then she gave him a saucer of creamy milk, and watched him while he drank it.

"What do you think of him?" asked Jean, anxiously.

"Well, my dear, he's a real beauty!" said Great-Aunt Jane. "You must surely have taken great care of him to make him so sturdy and sleek!"

"Oh, do you really think he's beautiful?" asked Jean in delight.

"Do you know what he is?" asked Great-Aunt Jane suddenly. "He's a golden tabby, and one of the finest I ever saw! I had two once, but they weren't nearly as lovely as your Goldie!"

Jean could hardly believe her ears.

She suddenly hugged Great-Aunt Jane,
then she hugged Goldie, and then she
hugged her great-aunt once more.

"Bless the child!" said Great-Aunt
Jane. "She thinks I'm a cat too, to have
all the breath squeezed out of me! Now
I've got an idea, Jean. Listen!"

"What?" asked Jean, breathlessly.

"There's a cat show to be held here in
a month's time," said Great-Aunt Jane.
"We'll enter your Goldie in the golden
tabby class, and see if he wins a prize!"

"Oh! Oh! Do let's!" squeaked Jean in
delight, hugging her great-aunt again.

"Jean! Do let me breathe!" said Great-Aunt Jane. "Well, if we do that you must keep Goldie very spick and span all month and brush him every day. You must see that he's fed well too. I will give you some money every week for him, so that Mummy won't be worried."

"You are a perfect dear," said Jean, hugging Goldie, instead of Great-Aunt Jane.

So it was all arranged. Great-Aunt Jane wrote to the cat show people and entered Goldie in the golden tabby class.

One day she gave Jean a big green ticket which had Goldie's name on it.

"Here you are," she said. "Next Saturday bring your Goldie here, and we'll put his cat show ticket on him. Then we'll all go to the show, and see what happens!"

Jean was so excited. She brushed Goldie every day, and fed him well and regularly. Mother got quite excited too, when she heard about it all.

At last the cat show day came.

Mother and Great-Aunt Jane, Goldie

and Jean, all went into the Town Hall, and found the place where Goldie was to sit that day.

Jean was so excited. Her knees kept shaking, so that she felt everyone must wonder what was the matter with her legs. When the judges came round to look at Goldie, she could hardly breathe.

And what do you think? Goldie won the first prize in the golden tabby class!

"He's a most beautifully shaped cat," one of the judges said to Jane. "And his colouring is lovely. Everything about him matches – his coat, his eyes, and his whiskers! Here's the first prize rosette for you. Hang it up by him!"

Jean couldn't say a word. She took the rosette, and hung it up for everyone to see. Her mother and Great-Aunt Jane were pleased.

"I told you so. I told you so!" said Great-Aunt Jane, banging the floor with her stick.

And when Jean went to get Goldie's prize, she found it was twenty-five pounds! She took Goldie up with her to get it, and everyone began to clap loudly.

But what Jean liked very nearly the best of all was when she carried Goldie over to Philip that evening.

"My word! What on earth is that rosette Goldie's got?" exclaimed Philip. "First prize! I say, Jean, how lovely!"

"Isn't it glorious?" said Jean, hugging Goldie, while he purred as loudly as a tiger. "And, oh Philip! This is his way of saying thank you for having saved him from drowning!"

And Goldie purred more loudly than ever, for Jean was quite right. He had been meaning to say thank you!

# Teapot
# Head

"There should be a king of this toy cupboard," said Teddy, who was trying to sound clever, as usual.

"And I suppose you think it should be you?" said the sailor doll, who was getting very tired of the teddy bear's high and mighty ways.

"It wouldn't be a bad idea," said Teddy, "I'm much cleverer than any of you. I deserve to be king. Look how I found out how to turn off the bathroom tap when somebody left it running. And look how I—"

"Do be quiet!" said the big doll. "We've all heard it before."

"Yes, but don't you think we should have a king?" said Teddy, who always went on and on about an idea once he had thought of one. "Don't you think we should—"

"Oh, listen to him!" groaned the sailor doll. "For goodness sake, Teddy, you can be king if you want to. We don't mind. Anything for the sake of a little peace and quiet!"

"Oooh!" said Teddy eagerly. "Do you really mean you'll have me as king?"

"I didn't say that," said the sailor doll. "I said you can be king if you like. We don't care. But you mustn't expect us to call you 'Your Majesty' or bow before you or do everything you tell us to."

"Then what's the good of me being king?" asked Teddy.

"I can't imagine," said the big doll. "Now do be quiet. We want to play snap."

Teddy thought about being king. It was very exciting. He would need a crown and cloak. He began talking again.

"Will you crown me?" he asked. "I'll need a crown. And I'll need a cloak, too."

"What's he talking about now?" said the sailor doll with a groan, looking up from the cards.

"I said, will you crown me and give me a cloak?" said Teddy impatiently. "You might listen when I say something."

The sailor doll looked at him and gave a sudden giggle. "All right. We'll crown you and give you a cloak tonight. The crowning will take place in front of the doll's-house. All the toys will attend."

Teddy was delighted. He had got his way and was going to have a crown and a cloak. He would be a real king and would have great fun ordering all the other toys about.

Teddy went to stand in front of the

doll's-house at the right time. All the toys were there too. The sailor doll had squeezed himself into the doll's-house to fetch something and there was a lot of giggling going on.

"Stand to attention, Teddy!" said the big doll as the sailor doll squeezed back out with a bedspread from one of the doll's beds, and a teapot from their tea-set. "You are about to be cloaked and crowned!"

Teddy stood up proudly. The sailor doll swung the bedspread round him. "Your cloak, sir!" he said grandly. Next he

clapped the teapot upside down on Teddy's head. "Your crown, sir!" he cried and everyone cheered loudly and laughed.

The teapot went right down over Teddy's face and hid his head completely. "Oh!" he cried. "My crown's too big!" But try as he might he just couldn't take that teapot off.

"I don't like this crown at all!" he shouted, his voice sounding strange coming out of the spout of the teapot. "I don't want to be king any more! Take it off! Please, take it off!"

But dear me, nobody could get it off. And there was poor old Teddy, with a teapot stuck fast on his head.

He wouldn't let anyone break it to get it off. "Alice will take it off when she notices it," he said. Alice was the little girl he belonged to. But she was away on holiday, and nobody knew when she was coming back. Poor old Teddy!

Of course nobody ever calls him 'Your Majesty'. They just say, "Oh, look, it's old Teapot Head," or, "Watch out, Teapot,

or you'll fall over our bricks!" or, "Don't you think Teapot's handsome now, with such a lovely spout for a nose?"

He's still got the teapot on but I expect Alice will notice it when she comes back after her holiday. You would if he was your bear, wouldn't you?

# The Red and Yellow Hoop

John had seen a ship in the toyshop window. It was a fine ship with a big white sail and it was called *The Seagull*. John badly wanted to buy it.

He emptied out his money-box. The ship cost three pounds and when he counted out his money he had just enough.

"Mummy, may I spend my money on a ship?" he asked. "I've got just enough. I've been saving for a long time."

"Yes, dear, if you like," said his mother. "Take Ann with you."

Ann was John's little sister. He was very fond of her, so he went to fetch her.

"Come along, Ann," he said. "I'm going to buy a ship at the toyshop. You can come with me, if you'd like to."

So off they went, running down the street, but just as they reached the toyshop, Ann fell over and cut her knee. She was frightened and began to cry. John felt sorry for her and bandaged up her knee with his handkerchief.

"Don't cry, Ann," he said. "Your knee will soon get better. Look! My handkerchief is wrapped round it."

But Ann wouldn't stop crying. She sobbed and sobbed and wanted her mother. John really didn't know what to do.

"Oh, Ann, please stop crying!" he begged. "Listen! I'll buy you something

at the toyshop if you like – but please stop crying!"

"Will you really buy me something?" she asked. "I thought you only had enough money for your ship."

"Never mind," said John. "I can save up again for the ship. I'll buy you something nice to make up for you hurting your knee."

It was very kind of John. He did badly want his ship, and he knew quite well that if he bought a toy for Ann he wouldn't have enough money to buy his ship as well. But he was very fond of his little sister and he wanted to comfort her.

The two of them went into the shop and Ann looked round. She didn't know what to choose.

Should it be a doll? Or a book? Or a toy train?

"Have you seen these lovely new hoops?" asked the shopkeeper, showing the little girl a heap of brightly coloured hoops. "Look, they are all painted different colours and they do look pretty

when you bowl them round and round.
The sticks are painted in all sorts of
pretty colours, too."

"Oh, yes, I'd like a hoop!" said Ann,
pleased. "I'll have a red and yellow one,
please. A nice big one, because I can run
fast."

"How much are they?" asked John,
feeling in his pocket for the money he
had brought, and trying very hard not to
look at the ship in the window.

"Three pounds, hoop and stick
together," said the shopkeeper. So John

paid him the money and he and Ann left the shop together. Ann was very happy. It really was a beautiful hoop, and she soon forgot about her hurt knee as she bowled her hoop along the road.

As they went along, they passed a river – and suddenly John heard a shout.

"Listen!" he said to Ann. "Was that a shout for help? Oh, I wonder if anyone has fallen into the river! Come quickly, Ann, and see!"

The two children rushed down to the riverside and looked in. They saw a little girl struggling in the water by herself. She had fallen in and couldn't get out. John couldn't swim, and the water was too deep for him to wade through. Whatever should he do? There was no one near to help. He must do something, or the little girl might drown.

Then a splendid idea came into his head. He called to Ann, who was looking very frightened. "Give me your new hoop, Ann. I believe if I hold it out to the little girl she can just reach it. Then together we can pull her to the bank!"

In a second Ann held out her hoop to John and he ran to the little girl. He caught hold of a tree nearby and then, leaning as far as he could over the water, he held out the brightly coloured hoop to the small girl.

"Catch hold!" he shouted. "Catch hold!"

The hoop just reached her! She put

out her hands and caught hold of it, pulling hard. John was nearly dragged into the water, too, but he held tightly to the tree, and Ann held him firmly round the waist.

"Hold tight!" shouted John, and the little girl in the water clung tightly to the hoop. Then John pulled hard and gradually he managed to drag the child towards the bank. The hoop stretched out of shape with the weight and, just as John put out his hand and dragged the little girl to safety, it snapped in half! But the girl was safe, and she climbed out quickly.

"Oh, thank you, thank you!" she cried. "It was a good idea to use your hoop like that. I'm so sorry it's broken. I'll ask my daddy to buy you a new one."

"That's all right," said John. "You'd better come home and get dry. We live quite near here. My mummy will dry you and give you some of Ann's clothes to wear."

So off they all went and soon she was being dried in front of the fire and John had been sent to tell the little girl's mother where she was.

Her mother and father came running to see if she was all right – and when they heard the story of the hoop, they were so grateful to Ann and John.

"You must come to tea tomorrow with Lucy," they said. "We will have a little party to show you how glad we are that you have saved our little girl."

The party was perfectly lovely – and, at the end of it, Lucy's mother brought out two big parcels, one for Ann and one for John. And what do you think was inside them?

Ann had another hoop, just like the one that had broken, and for John there was a wonderful sailing ship, far better than the one he had seen in the shop window. Wasn't he lucky!

"Well, you deserve it, John," said his mother when he got home. "You gave up your money to buy Ann a hoop when she fell down – and your kind deed has brought you something far better than the ship you were going to buy. I'm proud of you! You really do deserve your good luck."

# The Naughty
# Little Squirrel

Once upon a time there were two red squirrels. They were pretty creatures, with soft fur, big bushy tails, and lovely bright eyes. They lived together in the trees and had a big nest made of twigs, bark, moss and leaves. They had built it very strongly, and it was cosy and warm inside.

In the nest were four baby squirrels. They were just like their mother and father, but were not so big. They had not been much out of the nest, but each day the mother squirrel took them for a little scamper up and down the trees and then led them safely back to their nest.

One of the little squirrels was most adventurous. He wanted to go farther than his mother wished to take him.

"No, Bushy," she said to him. "You must not go any farther. You might meet a red fox on the ground – or a big kestrel might see you and pounce on you. Keep with me."

Frisky, Bobs and Tufty, the other little squirrels, were good and obedient. They did exactly as they were told. But Bushy really was naughty!

"If Mother won't let me go where I want to, I shall wait until we are left alone in the nest and then I shall jump out and go adventuring by myself!" he told the others.

"Don't be naughty, Bushy!" said Tufty.

"I shall be just as naughty as I feel like!" said Bushy. Wasn't he a rascal?

Now, the very next day the mother and father squirrel went to talk to some other squirrels in the trees at the other side of the wood. They leaped from bough to bough, as light as feathers, and were out of sight in a moment. Bushy poked his little head out of the nest.

"I'm off for an adventure!" he told his brothers and sisters – and off he went!

Down the tree he scampered and hunted about on the ground for a special toadstool his mother had told him about. He couldn't find one, so he scampered between the trees to see if he could find anything else nice to eat.

Suddenly he saw a big red creature watching him. The red animal had come silently out of a large hole.

The little squirrel looked at the big animal. It was a fox but he did not know it. He thought that the fox must be some sort of strange squirrel so he boldly said good morning.

"Good morning!" said the fox, his eyes gleaming as he watched the fat little squirrel bounding about. "Would you like to pay a visit to my home?"

"Where do you live?" asked the squirrel.

"I live under the ground," said the fox.

"What a strange place to live!" said the little squirrel in surprise. "My home is up in the trees!"

"My home is very cosy," said the fox. "Do come to dinner with me, squirrel. You look hungry."

"I am hungry!" said Bushy, feeling rather excited to think that such a big creature should be so nice and polite to him. "I will come with you."

"You go first!" said the fox, and he waved his paw to his hole. Bushy scampered over to pop down it – but suddenly he heard a little barking noise overhead, from the trees. He looked up. It was his mother, peeping down at him in fright.

"Bushy! Bushy! That's a fox! He will eat you for his dinner! Run quickly!"

The fox gave a snarl of anger and ran at Bushy. But the frightened little squirrel whisked round and scampered off. The fox raced after him.

"Run up the tree-trunk as I have taught you to!" called his mother. Bushy scampered up – but the fox snapped at his tail and took two or three hairs out of the tip! What a narrow escape for poor Bushy!

His mother took him back to the nest. "You see what happens to naughty, disobedient squirrels," she scolded. "If I had not come by just then you would have gone down the fox's hole and been eaten. You may think you are a clever, adventurous squirrel, but you are not. You are very stupid. Wait till you know more of the world before you run off alone like that!"

Poor Bushy! He settled down at the bottom of the nest and didn't say a word. He was frightened and ashamed. His tail hurt. He had very nearly lost it!

"I won't go out by myself until my mother says I may!" he thought. And after that he was just as good and obedient as the others were. He did have a narrow escape, didn't he?

# The Big Fur Monkey

There was once a very handsome monkey. He was made of pink fur and he had fine glass eyes, a long pink tail, and a most beautiful spotted bow. The inside of his ears was green, and he could squeak very loudly if you pressed him in the middle.

He lived on the bottom shelf in the toyshop, and he was very proud of himself indeed, for he was the biggest and best monkey in the shop. He cost a lot of money – so much that nobody bought him for a long time.

All the toys knew him well and were a little afraid of him because he was so grand. They didn't like him very much because he was boastful.

"When I'm sold I shall go to live in a palace, I expect," he often used to say.

"I shall belong to a rich little girl or boy and I shall be treated with great care and given a doll's bed to lie on and an armchair of my own. Ah, you poor toys, you don't know how grand I shall be!"

"And we don't care either," said the brown teddy bear, who was very tired of hearing all the monkey's boasting.

The monkey frowned and said no more. He thought the other toys were not worth talking to.

One day a rich little girl came into the shop with her granny. All the toys sat straight up and looked at her – but she didn't look so very nice. She had a sulky face and was always rude to people.

"Now which toy would you like?" said her granny kindly. "It's your birthday, so you can choose whichever you like."

"I want something that costs a lot of money," said the little girl.

"Well, here is a doll. She costs nineteen pounds," said the shop woman, taking down a pretty, golden-haired doll.

"I've got lots of dolls, thank you," said the little girl, looking round the shop.

"What about that pink monkey? I don't have a monkey at home. How much does he cost?"

"He costs twenty-five pounds," said the woman. "He is a very beautiful monkey."

"I want him, Granny," said the little girl. "He looks very pretty. He can sleep in my doll's cot at night, and I've a nice little deckchair that will just fit him."

Well, you should have seen how the pink monkey swelled with pride when he heard that! Hadn't he always said he would be bought by a rich little girl and live in a grand house and be treated well?

Now all the toys could see that he was right!

The shop woman wrapped him up and the little girl took him home. She sat him in her small deckchair and he felt very grand. He looked round at the other toys in the playroom. They seemed very old and battered.

"I don't think much of you!" said the monkey in disgust. "What dreadful, broken things you look!"

"Well, you won't look much better soon," said a doll with a broken nose. "You've no idea what a horrible little girl Mary is! She throws us about, stamps on us and breaks us whenever she is in a bad temper – which is nearly every day!"

"Good gracious!" said the monkey in alarm. "Well, I won't stand such behaviour!"

The very next day, when Mary came into the playroom, she was in a bad temper and began to throw her toys about. She took the monkey from his chair and trod on him! He squeaked loudly, of course, and the little girl heard

him and jumped up and down harder and harder, making him squeak more and more loudly.

At last his squeak broke and he could make no more noise. Then Mary flung him out of the window and he fell into the street below, right in the gutter.

It was muddy. The poor monkey lay half in water, and felt himself getting wet. He was very unhappy. To think that he, the most beautiful monkey that lived in the toyshop, should have been stamped on, and then flung into the gutter! He could have cried out loud with shame.

Presently an old woman came along. She saw the monkey lying there in the wet gutter, and she picked him up.

"Some child's dropped you, I suppose," she said. "Well, you aren't much to look at, all dirty and wet. I'll take you home and dry you and, if you're worth it, which seems unlikely, I'll give you away to someone."

She stuffed him into her basket with potatoes and cabbages. The potatoes made him dirtier than ever, and a large green caterpillar crawled out of a cabbage and on to his nose. It was dreadful. At last the old woman arrived home. She emptied her bag out on to the table.

"Good gracious!" she said, when she saw how dirty the toy monkey was. "You're not fit to be given away at all. I'd better put you into the dustbin straight away." The monkey could hardly believe his ears. Put into the dustbin! A monkey like him, who had cost twenty-five pounds and been the finest toy in the shop! He tried to squeak angrily, but his squeak was broken.

After a while the old woman picked him up and looked at him. "I'll just give you a wash," she said. "Maybe you won't look quite so bad then."

To the monkey's horror, she held him under a hot-water tap and nearly scalded him, the water was so hot. Then she shook him well, squeezed him, and took him out into the garden. She took two pegs and pegged the poor wet monkey up on to the clothes-line by his ears!

He was so ashamed, so very unhappy. To think that he, such a grand monkey, should have come to this!

The sun came out and warmed him. The wind blew and dried him. His fur had gone hard and tangled, his ears were out of shape, his tail was loose. He really was a funny sight.

The old woman came out and unpegged him. She brushed him hard with a clothes-brush and then looked at him. "Well," she said, "you're not much to look at, but I dare say Mrs Brown's children will be pleased to have you. There are six of them and they only have two toys between them! I'll take you along to them this very minute!"

Off she went with the monkey. He trembled when he thought of six children with so few toys.

What would happen to him now? He would be stamped on, thrown about, struck, smacked . . . oh, dear, what a dreadful fate!

The six children were delighted to see the monkey. The eldest child of the six was nine, the youngest was one.

"Oh, isn't he just beautiful!" cried Peter.

"Isn't he nice and cuddly!" shouted Mollie.

"I do love him! He's wonderful!" said little John.

"I want him for my own!" said Eileen. Nobody was rough with him. Everybody stroked him and made a fuss of him.

"You shall each have him for a day and a night in turn," said Mrs Brown, their mother. "He is a nice monkey and you must treat him well."

So each child had the monkey for a day and a night. First Peter played with him, took him out and showed him proudly to all the other children in the street – and at night he took the monkey to bed and cuddled him lovingly. Then Mollie had her turn and then all the others.

The monkey was very happy. He had lost his grand ideas, and had forgotten to be boastful and vain. The children loved him and he loved them. He didn't mind living with them at all, they were so kind to him. Nobody ever stamped on him. Nobody threw him out of the window as Mary had done.

One day he lost a glass eye and Mrs Brown sewed a black boot-button in its place. He looked a bit strange, but the children loved him just the same. Another time he lost half his tail and an ear – but still the children thought he

was the most beautiful monkey in the whole world. He slept in bed each night with one of them and was always being cuddled.

It happened one morning that the children took him into the park. There was another child there, with his mother, and this child had a teddy bear which was sitting on the seat while the little boy played. The Brown children put their monkey on the seat by the bear. They looked at one another.

"Why, aren't you the brown teddy bear that lived in the shop with me?" cried the monkey.

"Yes," said the bear, looking in astonishment at the poor battered monkey. "But it can't really be you, Pink Monkey! You look dreadful! I thought at least you had gone to live in a palace with a rich little girl – but here you are with a pack of dirty children, even dirtier than they are! You've a boot-button eye and only one ear! I am ashamed to be seen talking to you! Aren't you ashamed to be owned by such children?"

The monkey laughed.

"Oh, I was foolish in my young days!" he said. "I had a bed of my own, and a chair, and a rich little girl to play with – but I had no love, no kindness. These children may be poor and dirty, but they know how to be kind, they know how to love. I love them too. I don't want to be grand any more, I don't want to live with a rich little girl! The only things that matter, Brown Bear, whether you are a child or a toy, are love and kindness, and just you remember that! I love others and make them happy, and they love me and make me happy. What more can

anyone want than that?"

"You are wrong and foolish!" said the bear, turning away his head. "I really don't think I wish to talk to a dreadful-looking creature like you."

But all the same the pink monkey was right, wasn't he? Those children have still got him, and though he has lost all his tail now, and isn't in the least bit pink any longer, he doesn't care. He is still cuddled and loved, so he is perfectly happy; poor old battered fur monkey!

# I Shall
# Sit Here

There was once a daisy seed that flew on the wind and came to rest in a garden. It fell on a lawn where the children played, and settled down there. It put out a tiny root and a tiny shoot, and began to grow. The shoot grew two little leaves that reached up into the sunshine.

Then the grass round about spoke crossly: "Get away from here, daisy plant! A lawn is a lawn, and should only be grass. Daisies and clover and thistles are not welcome here. Get away and grow somewhere else."

"I can't," said the daisy. "Don't be unkind. I haven't runners like the strawberry plants have, that can run about all over the place, growing new little strawberry plants where they like.

I want to be here. It's a children's lawn, and children like daisies better than grass."

"Well, we shall grow thickly round you and smother you with hundreds of our little green blades," said the grass. "We shall stop you getting the light and the sun, and you will die!"

So the grass grew closely all round the tiny daisy plant, and it had hardly any room to grow at all. It was very upset, and called to a tiny ladybird running by.

"What can I do to grow safely in this lawn? The grass is trying to choke me!"

"I'll go and ask the thistles I know," said the ladybird, spreading her wings out. "There are some growing on the tennis lawn, though they know they are not allowed there. I'll see how they manage it."

In a few minutes the ladybird was back. "The thistle says it's quite easy. You are to sit down hard on the lawn, spread out your leaves firmly in a rosette, and tell the grass you are going to stay there," she said.

"Oh, thank you," said the daisy. "I'll do what you say."

Its leaves were now well grown. It had been holding them up in the air, out of the way of the grass, but now it put them down firmly on the grass itself. It arranged them cleverly in a rosette all

round itself, so that the grass blades beneath could not get any air or light, and had to move themselves away from the daisy.

"I shall sit here," said the little plant to the grass around. "I shall spread out my leafy skirts and sit down here. This is my own little place. Keep away, grass, or I shall sit on you!"

The grass grumbled, but it couldn't do anything about it! It had to keep away from the firm rosette of daisy leaves, or be smothered!

The daisy sent up tight little round buds, which opened in the sun. They spread out pink-tipped petals, with a round golden eye at the centre.

"That is how I get my name – day's eye – daisy!" said the daisy.

The children found the little daisy plant as they sat on the lawn, playing.

"Oh, look!" said Peter. "Daisies! Let's pick some, and put them in a tiny vase for Mummy."

"Yes, let's," said Jane. "I love daisies. They seem to look at us with their golden

eyes. I'm glad there are some on our lawn. I'm surprised the grass lets them grow here!"

"Aha!" thought the daisy. "I know the trick of growing in grass now. All I need to do is to say 'I shall sit here' and arrange my leaves in a rosette – then I can grow anywhere!"

It's quite true – that's what a daisy plant always does. You look and see the next time you are out in your garden!

# They Met
# Mr Pink-Whistle

In Breezy Wood there was a lovely little glade, with trees that were easy to climb, and a little pond that rippled in the breeze.

One of the trees had a low branch. It was strong enough to take three children at once, and they could swing up and down, up and down, as long as they liked. All the children liked doing that, even the big ones.

Five children came down to play in the little glade every Saturday. They were all small – three girls and two boys. Jean, Kitty, Alice, John and Eric. They sailed their boats on the shallow little pond, swung on the tree-branch, and climbed the trees.

And then one day two big boys found

the little glade. They looked around in delight.

"Just the place for us!" said Roy. "Trees to climb – water to paddle in – somewhere to make a campfire!"

"We'll find a hole in one of these trees, and make it a hiding-place for our boats and sweets and balls," said Terry. "And it shall be our glade – nobody else's!"

So they put up a notice on one of the trees: PRIVATE. KEEP OUT!

When the five children got there on the next Saturday, they saw the notice. "What does it mean?" said Alice. "This place isn't private! It's for anyone!"

"I shall take the notice down," Eric said boldly. So he did. Then they began their games as usual, swinging on the low branch and sailing boats on the pool.

Now, very soon Terry and Roy came along, carrying the things they meant to hide in the old hollow tree. They heard the shouts of the children as they came, and they were angry.

"Kids! And they've taken our notice down – look!" said Terry. "Let's chase them away."

"Well – there are five of them," said Roy, who was not very brave. "And anyway, they'll come back as soon as we've gone. We want this place for our very own."

The boys looked at one another. "Let's frighten them with some tale or other," said Roy. "We'll pretend there are some escaped bears or something hiding in this wood, in the glade or nearby. They'll rush off soon enough then!"

"All right. Let's pretend we've been chased by bears," said Terry with a giggle. "We'll scare the silly kids properly.

Come on now – yell and scream and rush about!"

So the five small children playing happily in the glade suddenly stopped in alarm when they heard fearful yells and screams coming from the bushes not far off. They heard the sound of running feet, then more yells.

"He's nearly got me! Help! The biggest bear I ever saw!"

"Save me! Save me! There's a big snake after me!"

It was only Terry and Roy, of course, pretending to be frightened just to scare the children. They suddenly ran into the glade, yelling, and the children almost jumped out of their skins!

"Run! Run! There are some escaped animals here!" cried Roy. "Don't come back here. It's dangerous. They may have their dens in this glade. Run for your lives!"

The children ran. Kitty cried as she went, and Jean caught her foot on a root and fell flat on her face. She yelled as she got up and ran again. They were all very frightened.

But after a week or two they forgot their fright, and thought that whatever escaped animals there were must surely have been caught by now.

"We'll go back to the glade," said John. "We'll go carefully, and look about. I told my mother about the escaped bears and snakes, and she only laughed. I'm sure it's safe."

So the five children went cautiously back to the glade they liked so much. Roy and Terry were there. They had built a little fire, and were roasting potatoes in it. Roy saw the children first, and nudged Terry.

"Here are those kids again. Shin up a tree quickly, and make some noises."

Up they went, and were well hidden by the time the five children came along.

"Someone's made a fire here – and that's forbidden," said Jean. "I'll stamp it out."

She stamped on it – and that made Roy feel very angry. He sent out a fierce, deep growl. Terry did the same, and the five children stood still in sudden fright.

"What was that?" whispered John. "It sounded like a growl."

"Would it – would it be a bear?" asked Kitty fearfully.

Then Roy decided to hiss like a snake. "S-s-s-sssssssss!"

"That was a snake!" cried Alice. "They're still here, the snakes and the bears. Quick, run!"

Such fierce growls and enormous hisses came at that moment that all five children took to their heels and fled. They ran and they ran – and at last came to the stile they had to climb over to get into the lane.

A little man was just about to get over the stile. He looked in surprise at the five panting, frightened children. Kitty was crying loudly.

"What's the matter?" said the little man. He was Mr Pink-Whistle, a little fellow who is half human and half a brownie. He goes about the world putting wrong things right, as everyone knows. Dear, dear – surely there was something very wrong here!

John told him all about the two boys who had warned them of the bears and snakes – and how, when they had gone back to the glade that morning they had heard growls and hisses, and had run for their lives.

Mr Pink-Whistle guessed at once that there was some horrid trick, of course. He wiped Kitty's eyes, and took some sweets from his pocket. "Now you all go off and play somewhere else," he said. "Take these sweets with you. Come back to the glade this afternoon, and you will

see a notice up. It will say 'All safe here', and you will know I've cleared away anything that shouldn't be there."

"Oh, thank you," said the children, and Kitty began to smile again. They went off together, looking back at Mr Pink-Whistle and thinking what a kind little man he was.

Now Mr Pink-Whistle, being half a brownie, could make himself invisible if he wanted to – and just at that minute he wanted to very badly. So, hey presto – he vanished, and only his shadow lay behind him, moving along as he walked towards the glade.

The two boys were there, lighting their fire again and giggling as they thought of the scared children.

"Didn't they run!" said Terry. "Don't you think I growled well?"

"Well, what about my hissing?" said Roy. "I'm sure no snake ever hissed louder!"

"Fancy believing our silly stories about bears and things," said Terry. "As if escaped animals would live in this glade!"

Mr Pink-Whistle decided it was about time that he began his performance. Aha! He could imitate any animal under the sun – bears, lions, snakes, wolves, hyenas!

He was invisible. He could move where he liked, the two boys couldn't see him. He went to a nearby tree and shook a branch violently as if some animal was hiding there. And he grunted – grunted like a big grizzly bear.

Roy and Terry looked up at once. "What was that?"

"Something grunting – in that tree," said Roy. But by now the tree had stopped swishing about, and Mr Pink-Whistle had gone to a small bush. He crawled underneath, making the branches move, and began roaring. You should have heard him! Why, even the lions at the zoo would have listened in astonishment.

Terry clutched Roy in great alarm. "What is it? Something different now. It's hiding under that bush. It sounds – oh, Roy, it sounds like a lion!"

"Let's run," said Roy. But they couldn't. They just couldn't move, they were so scared. Mr Pink-Whistle came out from the bush and went quietly over beside the boys. They couldn't see him, of course, because he was still invisible.

He stroked their legs and hissed. What a hiss! "Sssssssssss!" Just like that.

"Snakes – round our legs! Where are they? I can't see them!" yelled Roy, and he was so frightened that he sat down suddenly. His legs wouldn't bear him any longer. Mr Pink-Whistle decided to change his stroking and hissing into galloping and neighing.

So the two boys then had to listen to feet apparently galloping round the glade, and a great neighing, as if three or four horses were there together.

"They'll gallop over us!" cried Roy – and then the galloping stopped, and a quacking began.

"Quack, quack, quack! Quack, quack, quack!"

"Ducks – but there aren't any here!" said Roy, almost crying. "Let's go, let's go! It's like a bad dream."

A howl like a dog's came right in his ear, and he leaped to his feet. He yelled – and he ran. My word, how he ran! He would have won all the running races in his school sports if he had been running in them at that moment!

Terry ran too, stumbling as he went, looking fearfully at every bush and tree for some animal in hiding. They didn't stop running till they came to the stile. Then, panting and exhausted, they climbed to the top, and sat there, looking back over the field towards the glade.

A little man appeared beside them, and they jumped. It was Mr Pink-Whistle, of course, not invisible any longer.

"Oh! You made me jump! I didn't see you coming," said Roy.

"You seem rather alarmed about something," said Mr Pink-Whistle, beaming at them. "What's the matter?"

"Well – we've heard bears – and lions – and horses galloping, and ducks – over in that glade," said Roy, shaking, as he thought of them.

"Dear me," said Mr Pink-Whistle. "Some small children I met this morning told me about them. They ran, too. They said two boys had warned them that there were escaped animals about.

Perhaps you were the two boys who so
kindly told them?"

"Er – well – yes, we did say something
about animals and snakes," said Terry.
"We told the kids not to go to that glade."

"Then surely it was foolish of you to go
there, and light a fire?" said Mr Pink-
Whistle. "It was asking for trouble,

109

wasn't it? I mean – if you were so certain that there were bears and snakes there, why did you go?"

Terry and Roy didn't know what to say to that. They didn't want to tell this strange little man that they had told the children a lot of untruths just to get them out of the glade and make them afraid to come back.

A cow in a field nearby suddenly mooed. Roy almost fell off the stile.

"Dear, dear. Oh, how scared you are!" said Mr Pink-Whistle. "That was only the cow over there. Would you like to go back to that glade with me, and hunt for these animals you say are there?"

"No!" cried both boys at once, and they leaped off the other side of the stile at once. "No, oh, no!"

"I'll never go back to that glade as long as I live!" said Roy. "Never!"

"Nor will I!" said Terry, and they both ran off at top speed as if they were afraid that Mr Pink-Whistle would take them back with him! How he laughed to see them go.

"Now they know what it's like to be scared," he said. "Maybe they won't frighten small children again. Well – I enjoyed that, though I've made my throat a bit sore with all that roaring."

And off went little Mr Pink-Whistle down the road. One more thing put right – a very good morning's work.

That afternoon the five children went cautiously to the wood once more. The

first thing they saw was a big notice on the hollow tree, which said: ALL SAFE HERE.

"Hurrah!" they said. "Now we can play here again. That kind little man has chased the animals away. Who could he have been?"

Well – we could tell them, couldn't we?

# The Sticky Gnome's Prank

The sticky gnome walked along the little path that ran over Bumble-Bee Common, humming a merry tune. It was a fine sunny day and he felt happy. In his left hand he carried his pot of brown glue and under his right arm were three brushes.

Sticky went about gluing broken things for people. His glue was very strong and could mend things and make them as good as new. He made it himself and he was very proud of it.

Now as he went along the little grassy path he saw a pair of shoes and a top hat lying beside a gorse bush. He was surprised to see them there and he looked about to see whose they were. And, on the other side of the bush, he

saw a fat gnome lying down fast asleep.

Sticky stood looking at him, wondering who he was. He was dressed in a blue silk coat and bright yellow trousers, so he looked very smart.

As Sticky looked at the sleeping gnome a naughty thought came into his head, and he grinned a wicked grin. He dipped one of his brushes into his pot of glue, and stirred it round until it was covered with the sticky mess. Then he carefully painted the rim of each empty shoe, and, turning up the top hat, he painted the inside of that, too! Then he stood back and laughed to himself. There stood the gnome's shoes side by side, and there was the top hat – all neatly brushed with the stickiest glue in the whole kingdom.

"Now I must wake him up and see him put them on!" thought Sticky, chuckling. So he went behind the bush and shouted as loudly as ever he could, "Hey! Hey! Hey!"

The sleeping gnome woke up with a jump and sat up in a hurry. He looked all round to see where the shouting had come from.

"I wonder what woke me," he said. "I am sure I heard someone shouting. What's the time? Dear, oh, dear, it's already twelve o'clock! I shall never be in time to meet the dear prince!"

With that he slipped on his shoes as quickly as he could, and put his top hat firmly on his head. How the naughty sticky gnome chuckled to himself to see him!

"I'll follow him and see what happens

when he tries to take off his hat," said Sticky. So he followed the fat gnome as closely as he could without being seen. He soon saw that the gnome was going to the station to meet the prince he had spoken of.

"Then he'll have to take off his hat, and he won't be able to," said the wicked little gnome, dancing in delight to think of the naughty trick he had played. Now on the way to the station the fat gnome got a stone in one of his shoes. So, of course, he bent down to take it off so that he might shake out the stone. And then, to his enormous astonishment, he found that he couldn't pull the shoe from his foot. It stuck there as tightly as could be!

The fat gnome pulled and tugged at it. No use at all! The shoe wouldn't move at all.

"Extraordinary!" said the gnome, in amazement. "What's the matter with it? It's never been like this before. I'll try the other shoe and see if that will come off."

But of course it wouldn't. It was stuck

as tightly as the other one. The poor fat gnome was in an awful state about it. He looked at his watch and found that it was really getting very late indeed. He would have to go to the station as fast as ever he could. So off he hobbled, limping badly because the stone hurt him. Sticky followed, keeping out of sight, for he felt sure that the gnome would be very angry with him if he guessed what had happened.

The train was in the station when the fat gnome got there. The prince was looking all round, and he was annoyed not to see anyone to meet him. As soon as he saw the fat gnome he went up to him and shook him by the hand – and, to the Prince's great surprise, the gnome didn't take off his top hat to him!

The poor gnome certainly tried to – but his hat was stuck as tightly as his shoes and he couldn't lift it at all. It was most alarming.

"Why don't you take off your hat when you greet me?" the prince asked crossly.

"I'm really very sorry," said the poor gnome, as red as a tomato, "but I can't seem to get it off."

"Then you should wear a larger size," snapped the prince. "Come along, let's walk to your house. I don't want to ride. It's such a nice walk over Bumble-Bee Common."

So off they went together, the prince and the gnome. But the gnome still had a stone in his left shoe and he limped very badly.

"What's the matter with your foot?" asked the prince, quite annoyed to find the gnome hobbling along so slowly.

"There's a stone in one of my shoes," said the gnome, humbly. "I'm very sorry."

"Well, take it out then!" said the prince.

"I can't," said the gnome. "My shoes are stuck as hard as my hat. I'm so sorry, Prince – but I can't really think what has happened."

"Perhaps it's a spell," said the prince, and he knelt down to look at the gnome's shoes. He pushed a finger into one and looked up at the gnome.

"Someone's played a trick on you," he said. "There is glue inside your shoes – and very strong, sticky glue it is, too! Let me put my finger under your hat – yes, that's sticky too! Dear, dear, who's been playing pranks on you, I'd like to know?"

The sticky gnome was chuckling to see all that was happening – he had hidden behind a bush and was peeping out to see. But he didn't know that the prince was a powerful enchanter! Before half a minute had passed the prince had called out a string of magic words to bring before him the one who had played such a wicked prank on the poor, fat gnome – and to Sticky's fright and alarm he found himself being forced to run right up to the prince and the gnome, taking his glue and all of his brushes with him!

"Oho! So you're the one who has done this, are you?" said the prince, peering into the pot and seeing the glue there. "Come here!"

He took hold of Sticky, dipped a brush

in the glue-pot and began pasting him
with the glue from head to foot! Sticky –
and he really was very sticky now –
howled dismally. The fat gnome looked
on in astonishment. Then he rolled up
his sleeves and said, "Let me have a turn,
Prince! I'd like to do a bit of pasting, too.
There's more than one brush, and I will
make him beg to be let off and promise
never to be naughty again!"

But when Sticky saw the gnome dip
another brush into the glue-pot, he was

frightened and fled away as fast as ever he could, with his pot of glue and his brushes. The fat gnome ran after him for a long way and only gave up the chase when he saw Sticky running through the gates of Fairyland and into our world.

Sticky is still with us – do you know what he does? He paints all the chestnut buds with glue, and makes the lime trees sticky in the summer. He gives some of his glue to the spiders for their webs – so it's no wonder they are so sticky, is it? Perhaps you will see him some day if you keep a sharp look-out.

# Ho-Ho
## Plays a Trick

There was great excitement in the Village of Bo. Old Mother Tippy's cottage had caught fire and had burned down to the ground. Mother Tippy had only been able to save two chairs and her bed, so the poor old dame was very sad and upset.

But the brownies of Bo came round and comforted her. "We will all give you what money we can spare!" they promised. "Then you will be able to get another cottage and buy what furniture you like!"

Ho-Ho said he would go round and collect money from every brownie in the village.

"But you won't get a penny piece from that mean old miser, Snip-Snap!" said Gobo, grinning. "Nobody has ever known him to give any of his money away!"

"Well, I'll try anyway," said Ho-Ho cheerfully. "He's rich enough to give me ten gold coins, goodness knows!"

Then off went the little brownie with a large collecting-box, to get as much money as he could for old Mother Tippy.

When he came to the cottage where Snip-Snap lived he heard a sound of angry shouting and he stopped. The brownie who lived next door poked his head out of the window, and called to Ho-Ho.

"Are you collecting money for Mother Tippy? Well, here is mine – but I warn you – don't go near Snip-Snap today, whatever you do! He's in a most furious temper. Can't you hear him shouting?"

"Yes," said Ho-Ho, listening. "What's the matter with him?"

"You know that beautiful brooch he wears on the front of his jersey?" said the brownie. "It's a very magic brooch, and he thinks a great deal of it. Well, it's either lost or stolen! He looked down at his jersey this morning, and it wasn't there! He's hunted all through his house to find it and he can't, so he thinks a thief must have taken it."

"Well, I haven't taken it," said Ho-Ho. "I shall go and ask him to put something in my box for poor old Mother Tippy."

So, very bravely, he went up to the door of Snip-Snap's cottage and knocked loudly. The door flew open and there stood the old miser, his eyes gleaming fiercely, and his hair flying about all over his big head.

"What is it, what is it?" he snapped. "Have you brought me news of my stolen brooch?"

"No," said Ho-Ho. "I've come to ask you to give me some money to help poor Mother Tippy, whose cottage was burned down last night."

"Stuff and nonsense!" said Snip-Snap, rudely. "What do I care for that silly old woman? I'm much too busy this morning with my own troubles to bother about other people's. I never did like that old woman, anyway!"

"Don't be so unkind!" said Ho-Ho. "She is in great trouble. You are a mean old miser, Snip-Snap, and I hope you never find your brooch! So there!"

Snip-Snap was full of rage when he heard this. He lifted up his fist and struck out angrily at Ho-Ho. But the small brownie ducked his head, and Snip-Snap spun round in the air, and fell down in a heap on his front door mat. In a flash he jumped up and slammed the door in Ho-Ho's face.

Ho-Ho went down the path, grinning

as he thought of how funny Snip-Snap
had looked whirling and tumbling down
on his mat. As he remembered this, he
suddenly stopped and scratched his head.
What was it that he had caught sight of
on Snip-Snap's back as he fell? It was
something bright and glittering!

Ho-Ho slapped his knee and laughed

aloud. "Ho-ho-ho! Ha-ha-ha! Now I know what has happened to Snip-Snap's precious brooch! The silly fellow has put his jersey on back to front, so of course his brooch is at the back today, and he can't see it. Ho-ho-ho!"

Ho-Ho laughed till the tears ran down his cheeks. Then he wiped them away and began to think. Couldn't he play a little trick on mean old Snip-Snap? Couldn't he somehow manage to get a lot of money out of him for Mother Tippy? He thought he could!

After a while he went back up the path to Snip-Snap's front door and knocked again, this time twice as loudly as before.

Snip-Snap put his head out of an upstairs window and roared, "Who is it now? What do you want? Go away!"

"Please, Snip-Snap, it's me again," said Ho-Ho.

Snip-Snap made a noise like a railway train going through a tunnel, and nearly fell out of the window with rage.

"Grrrr!" he roared. "I'll turn you into a black-beetle and tread on you, you

nasty, twisty-toed little nuisance!"

"I may be nasty, but I'm not twisty-toed, Snip-Snap!" said Ho-Ho, cheerfully. "I've only just come back to say that I know who's got your brooch. But if I'm a nuisance to you, I'll go. Goodbye!"

"Wait, wait!" yelled Snip-Snap, at once. "Tell me who has my brooch! The thief, the robber! Aha, wait till I get him, and I'll send him flying to the moon!"

"Oh, I wouldn't do that; you might be sorry!" said Ho-Ho, grinning.

"Nothing's too bad to do to the nasty person who has my precious brooch!"

said Snip-Snap. "Quick, tell me!"

"I'll make a bargain with you, Snip-Snap," said Ho-Ho. "If I tell you who has your brooch and where it is, will you put ten gold coins into my collecting-box to give to old Mother Tippy?"

"You must be mad!" cried Snip-Snap. "Whoever would think of giving ten gold coins to that silly old woman!"

"Well, I would, for one, if I had them to give," said Ho-Ho. "But never mind, Snip-Snap – if you don't want to make a bargain with me, I'll go. I've a lot of collecting to do this morning."

Ho-Ho turned himself about as if he were going away. Snip-Snap gave a yell, slammed down the window and rushed down his stairs, four steps at a time. He flung open his front door and called to Ho-Ho. "Stop! Stop! I'll give you five gold coins if you will tell me who has my magic brooch!"

"I said ten!" said Ho-Ho, going down the path and opening the gate.

"Don't be silly," said Snip-Snap. "I can't possibly give you ten."

"Well, of course, if your brooch isn't worth ten gold coins, I can't expect you to give it," said Ho-Ho. "So I won't waste any more of my time or yours, Snip-Snap. Good morning!"

He slammed the gate shut. Snip-Snap tore down the path after him.

"I'll give you eight gold coins!" he cried.

"TEN!" roared Ho-Ho, who was thoroughly enjoying himself. He could see all the brownies who lived on either side, poking their heads out of their windows and grinning from ear to ear.

What fun it was to play a trick on mean old Snip-Snap!

"Nine gold coins!" said Snip-Snap, in despair.

"TEN!" yelled Ho-Ho.

"Oh, very well," said Snip-Snap, sulkily, giving way suddenly. "I'll make it ten gold coins – but it's robbery, sheer robbery!"

"Not at all," said Ho-Ho, holding out his collecting-box to Snip-Snap. "Not robbery at all – just a very generous gift from you to Mother Tippy – and very grateful she'll be, I'm sure!"

"I don't care tuppence about the old woman!" said Snip-Snap. "Here you are." He counted out the coins: "One-two-three-four-five-six-seven-eight-nine-ten – all pure gold! Now tell me who has my precious magic brooch and where it is!

Stars and moons, won't I give that thief a nasty surprise!"

"I don't think I would if I were you!" said Ho-Ho, with a wide grin. "Thanks so much for your generous help. Now I'll tell you where your brooch is and who has it. Come here, Snip-Snap!"

He took hold of the old miser and twisted him round. He undid the brooch from the back of his jersey and held it out to the astonished Snip-Snap with a polite bow.

"You had your brooch, and it was on your jersey as usual," he said. "But, dear Snip-Snap, you must have put your old jersey on back to front this morning. Goodbye, old fellow – and thanks again so very much for your ten gold coins for poor old Mother Tippy!"

Off skipped Ho-Ho, grinning all over his jolly little face, and the watching brownies roared with laughter to see the old miser, Snip-Snap, standing without a word to say, holding his precious brooch in his hand.

As for Mother Tippy, she was able to buy some beautiful new furniture, and now she lives in a pretty little cottage as happy as can be – but what puzzles her very much is how Ho-Ho managed to get such a lot of money from old Snip-Snap the miser!

Really, it was very clever of Ho-Ho, wasn't it?

# Mrs
# Tap-Tap-Tap

Nobody knew what the little old lady's real name was. Everybody called her Mrs Tap-Tap-Tap, because she always used to tap with a stick as she walked along.

You see, she was blind, and because she couldn't see, she had to take a stick with her wherever she went, to tap along the pavement to find the kerb.

She was a nice, cheery old lady, and she often went out for walks by herself, but she could never cross the road unless somebody helped her, because she couldn't see if any cars were coming.

The children were very good to her. As soon as any boy or girl saw Mrs Tap-Tap-Tap waiting at the kerb to cross the road, one of them would go up to her and take her arm. Then, as soon as the road was clear, they would take her safely across to the other side.

"Thank you, my dear," Mrs Tap-Tap-Tap would say, and off she would go on her way again, tap-tap-tapping with her stick.

One of the children who helped Mrs Tap-Tap-Tap a great deal was Johnny Watson. He always met her as he went home from afternoon school, and she often waited for him to help her across the road.

"Hello, Johnny!" she would say, as he came running up behind her. "I always know the sound of your feet."

"Hello, Mrs Tap-Tap-Tap!" Johnny would say. "Let me help you across the road. Wait a moment – there's a car. Now it's gone. We are safe."

This happened nearly every afternoon, and Johnny liked Mrs Tap-Tap-Tap very much, because she always had a joke for him.

Now one November afternoon a thick fog came down, and when Johnny came out from school he could hardly see the school gates. At first he thought it was fun. Then he didn't – because he found that everywhere looked so very different, and he began to feel that he didn't know the way back home.

"It's this way," he said to himself, and he felt along the railings nearby. "I should come to a corner here."

But he didn't. There didn't seem to be a corner anywhere. He went back again, and tried to find where the school gates were, to start off home again. But he couldn't find the gates!

"This horrible fog makes everything as dark as night," said Johnny, trying not to feel frightened. "Oh dear – wherever am I? I really don't know. I am quite lost."

He stood where he was for a little while, hoping that somebody would come along and he could ask them the way. But nobody came. Everyone was safe at home.

Johnny set off again, trying to read the names of the houses, so that he would know where he was. But it was too foggy even to do that.

At last he stood still again, thinking that he must be going even farther away from home instead of getting nearer. And then he heard someone coming!

*Tap-Tap-Tap! Tap-Tap-Tap!* That was the noise he heard.

"Goodness! It must be Mrs Tap-Tap-Tap's stick!" said Johnny. "Fancy her being out on a dreadful day like this! I hope she isn't lost too."

Presently Mrs Tap-Tap-Tap came right

by Johnny. He put out his hand and stopped her.

"Mrs Tap-Tap-Tap, are you lost too?" he asked.

"Lost!" said the old lady in surprise. "Of course not! Why should I be?"

"Well, it's as dark as night today, with this thick fog," said Johnny.

"Little boy. It is always as dark as night to me," said Mrs Tap-Tap-Tap. "Blind people are always in the dark, you know – so what's a fog to me? I know my way as well in a fog as I do in the sunlight."

"Do you really?" said Johnny, most

surprised. "I've never thought of that."

"Ah, Johnny, you may be able to get home all right in the daylight, but I'm cleverer then you in a fog," chuckled Mrs Tap-Tap-Tap. "It seems to me, Johnny, that I shall have to help *you* today! Well, that will be a pleasant change! Come along with me. My house is just near here. We'll have a cup of tea, and then I will take you home."

Johnny slipped his hand under the old lady's arm and went along with her. She knew her way well. She tap-tapped with her stick, turned the right corners, and knew just which way to go. At last she came to a little house. She took the key from her pocket and opened the door. In they went. A plump little lady came running up the hall. "I am glad to see you safe!" she cried.

"Safe as can be!" said Mrs Tap-Tap-Tap. "Now, Janet, please bring us tea and toast and some of my best shortbread. We have a visitor today – somebody who has helped me a lot at one time and another."

Soon Johnny and Mrs Tap-Tap-Tap were sitting down and eating a delicious tea. Then Mrs Tap-Tap-Tap put on her hat again and set off down the street with Johnny. It was still very foggy – but the old lady didn't mind about that. No – she could see as well in the dark as in the light!

It wasn't long before they came to Johnny's home. Johnny's mother was so glad to see him. She hadn't worried about him really, because she had thought he was staying to tea at school as it was so foggy. She thanked Mrs Tap-Tap-Tap very kindly for bringing Johnny home safely.

"Oh, Johnny has often done me a good turn," said the old lady, smiling. "Now it's my turn to do a good turn for him. Goodbye, Johnny! You'll see me across the road safely tomorrow if it's fine, won't you?"

"Of course I will!" said Johnny. "I will be your eyes on a sunny day – and you can be mine on a foggy one!"

# The Land
## of P's and Q's

Once upon a time there lived a little boy called Donald, who would never say "thank you". Sometimes he remembered "please", but only when he wanted something very badly, and thought he wouldn't get it unless he said "please". So you can see he wasn't a very polite little boy. This is the story of how he was cured.

Now one day Donald was playing by himself in a field at the back of his house. It was about eleven o'clock in the morning, and it suddenly seemed to Donald that he had had his breakfast a very long time ago.

"I'm so hungry!" he said. "Perhaps I'd better go home and see if it's lunch-time."

"No, don't do that!" said a voice over

the hedge. "Come and join us in our picnic, won't you?"

Donald looked over the hedge in surprise. He saw four little men dressed in red. They were sitting on the ground, eating enormous currant buns that had a delicious, freshly-baked smell.

"Oh!" said Donald, sniffing. "Your buns do smell good! I'd love to join you!"

Donald climbed over the hedge, and sat down beside the little men.

In the middle was a large dish of buns. The biggest man handed it politely to Donald. He took the very biggest one on

the dish, and began eating it, without saying a single "thank you".

"What a disgusting little boy!" said Rab, the chief little man in red, when Donald had eaten all his cake. "He can't even say 'thank you'. We must certainly try to cure him."

"Let's take him to the land of P's and Q's," said another little man. "He'll soon be cured then!"

Donald jumped up. "I won't go to that horrid country!" he cried. "I'm going home, so there!"

"All right. Just you try and go home!" said Rab.

Donald turned and tried to walk to the hedge. "Oh!" he cried, "my feet won't move! It's magic! Let me go!"

"No, you must come with us," said Rab, getting up. "We cure ever so many boys and girls who won't say 'please' or 'thank you'. You'll be much nicer when you come back."

Donald felt frightened. He was much too big to cry, of course, but he felt very like crying when the little men surrounded him, put their hands on his shoulders, and marched him off through the woods. They went right into the heart of the woods, until they reached a ring of very large toadstools.

"Sit down on one, Donald," said Rab, "and hold tight."

All the little men chose a toadstool, and sat down near Donald. Donald had a big toadstool, and held tight as Rab had told him.

"One, two, three, And down go we!" shouted Rab suddenly. Donald felt his toadstool sinking quickly into the ground, and he saw that all the others were too.

Down and down he went, seeing nothing at all, for it was quite dark. Then *bump*! His toadstool came to a stop in a great cave, lit by swinging blue lamps.

All the others were there too, and they jumped off their toadstools just as Donald did.

"Come on, Donald!" they cried. "This way!"

They led him through the blue cave, until they came to another cave, this time lit by green lamps. A pair of very small railway lines ran through it.

"Oh, a railway! Where does it go to?" asked Donald, astonished.

"All sorts of places!" answered Rab. "You can get to any part of Fairyland by Gnome Railway."

Suddenly a little engine came out of the darkness, pulling odd-looking carriages behind it. They had no roofs and no seats – just cushions on the floor for passengers to sit on.

"Jump in!" cried Rab, pushing Donald into a carriage as the train stopped. All the little men got in and chose cushions. Off went the train again.

After a long time, and after they had passed a lot of stations with strange-sounding names, the train left the caves and came out into the open air. Fiddlestick Field, Breezy Corner and Pool-in-the-Hollow were some of the stations that they went through, and Donald longed to get out and explore, for he knew he was in Fairyland. At some of the stations there were fairies and elves, pixies and gnomes, and they looked very exciting with their shining wings.

At last the train slowed down again. "P's and Q's! P's and Q's!" shouted a gnome porter.

"Jump out quickly, Donald!" said Rab. The little men jumped out, and Donald with them.

He found himself in a field of beautiful flowers, and just by him was a big signpost:

TO THE LAND OF P's AND Q's.

"Follow the path over the field," said Rab, "and go straight ahead. Go to the Yellow Castle and ask for Giant Politesse. He'll tell you what to do. You can go home again if you can find the Courteous Gate and go through it safely! I'll be waiting for you on the other side, and I'll take you home again."

The little men jumped into the waiting train, waved their hands, and off they went, leaving poor Donald alone.

**149**

Donald stared after them, feeling very lonely. When the train had disappeared from view, he went over the field, and came at last to a stile. In the distance he saw a big yellow castle on a hill.

"Oh, that must be the castle where Giant Politesse lives!" thought Donald. "I hope he'll be kind to me, and let me go home!"

When he arrived at the castle, he found the giant sitting outside the front door. He was a huge giant, with kind blue eyes and the most wonderful manners. Donald didn't feel at all afraid of him, and told him all about Rab, and how the little men in red had brought him to Fairyland.

"Oh, do let me go home!" he begged at the end.

"No, you can't go home till you've learned to be polite!" said Giant Politesse. "You must stay here awhile. Go to the kitchen, and ask my servants if they will have you as kitchen boy. They will teach you to be polite, and then you can go home."

Donald went sadly to the kitchen, where there was a great clattering of pots and pans. There were the strangest little beings there. Some of them were dressed in blue overalls and caps which had a big "P" embroidered on them. Some of them had purple overalls, and these had "Q" embroidered on them.

"I suppose these are the P's and Q's," thought Donald, standing and watching them.

Then he said out loud, "Can I be your kitchen boy, and help you?"

"Did Giant Politesse send you?" asked one.

"Yes," he said, "so do let me."

"Well, sit down," said the cook, "we're just going to have lunch."

Donald sat down at a long table and watched the cook ladling out meat and potatoes.

"Will you have a potato, Donald?" asked the cook.

"Yes, a big one," he answered, forgetting to say "please".

Then what do you think happened? The largest potato in the dish jumped straight out, flew to Donald, and hit him on the chest! And there it stayed!

"Oh, oh! Help!" yelled Donald, trying to get the potato off.

"You forgot to say 'please'," said the cook. "That sort of thing always happens in the Land of P's and Q's to anyone who forgets to be polite! You won't be able to get it off till you pass through the Courteous Gate on your way home."

It was quite true. That potato wouldn't come off, so Donald had to let it stay there. He was very upset about it.

"Here is your meat!" said the cook, handing the plate to Donald. He took it and set it down in front of him and – will you believe it – he didn't say "thank you".

Up jumped the meat, splashing the gravy all over Donald, and landing on his sleeve! There it stayed, and Donald couldn't get it off.

"Well, you are a little stupid!" cried the P's and Q's. "You forgot to say 'thank you'!"

Poor Donald nearly cried with frustration, he was so hungry and wanted his lunch. He was very careful to say "please" and "thank you" for his pudding and he ate it up hungrily.

After lunch, Donald helped to wash up all the plates. One dish was very sticky and horrid, and he could not get it clean.

"Give it to me; I'll do it for you," said a P kindly. Donald handed him the dish without a word. *Clap!* The plate jumped straight out of the P's hand, and landed on Donald's head!

"Oh! You didn't thank me for saying I'd help you!" exclaimed the P. "Now look what the plate's done!"

Well, Donald couldn't get that plate off, so you can imagine how strange he looked with a potato and some meat on his chest and sleeve, and a plate on his head.

"Oh dear, oh dear! I must be careful," cried Donald. "I'd no idea I forgot so often!"

He tried very hard to remember after that. The P's and Q's were very kind to him, and when he didn't know how to do anything, they would always show him. Donald thought they were very nice, and he began to think it would be rather jolly if he could be nice like that too!

It is hard to be nice with a cold potato sticking on your chest, and a stupid plate balanced on your head, but Donald managed it. He only forgot once, and that was when a Q came running in with a little grey kitten in his arms.

"Look!" he cried. "Here's a darling little baby kitten."

155

All the P's and Q's rushed to see. Donald rushed too, but he was last and could see nothing.

He pushed his way through to the front. "Let me see! Let me see!" he cried.

"Don't push! It's rude!" said the cook. Then, *swish*! the kitten jumped up on to Donald's shoulder, and stayed there.

"Now look what's happened!" cried a Q. "You were rude, and the little kitten will stay on your shoulder till you're polite! Poor little kitten!"

So Donald had to carry the little, mewing, scratching kitten on his shoulder all evening. He was very upset, because he felt that it was very unkind to the kitten as well as being uncomfortable for himself.

Donald lived in the castle for two or three days, trying hard to be as polite and kind as the P's and Q's. He tried to help them and to do all he could to make himself a really nice little boy.

He forgot to say "please" only once when he wanted some chocolate, and that jumped down his neck, and felt very

uncomfortable – and another time he took too much treacle with his pudding, and you can guess what he felt like when that jumped at him! He was sticky all day after that, for he couldn't get rid of it.

One morning Donald felt very tired, for the day before he had cleaned six pairs of Giant Politesse's boots, and as they were each quite as big as an ordinary bath, he had worked hard. He decided he would have a good rest the next morning, and do something easy.

"I'll clean the spoons!" he thought. So he sat down and began. But presently in came the cook, holding his head and moaning.

"Oh, oh! My head does ache! And I've got to go out in the hot sun, and tell the butcher to send the meat at twelve o'clock," moaned the cook.

"I'll go for you," said Donald, jumping up.

"But you're tired, and it's a long way!" said the cook.

"Never mind. I'll go for you!" said Donald. "Go and lie down, and perhaps you'll feel better."

"Well, it's very kind of you, and thank you very much!" said the cook. "Go down the road for a mile, then up Crooked Hill. The butcher lives at the top. Please give him my message, and tell him I couldn't come myself."

Off went Donald in the hot sun, down the road for a mile, and then over the fields to Crooked Hill. By the time he got there he was so tired he could hardly walk! He gave his message to the butcher, who seemed very much surprised to see a boy with a kitten, a potato, a plate and

meat all hanging about him.

"And please could you tell me a short way back?" asked Donald.

"Go down the hill, and over the stile," said the butcher. "That will be much shorter."

Donald thanked him and went down the hill, and over the stile. And what do you think he saw on the other side of the stile? Why, a great gate, and over it were these words:

THE COURTEOUS GATE.

It was shut. Donald peered through it and saw a blue plane in a field beyond the gate. Then he saw Rab, the little man in red, peeping through the gate at him.

"Are you cured yet?" asked Rab. "My! You do look funny! What a pity you've got a plate on your head, it looks so strange!"

"Please open the gate, and let me through," begged Donald.

"Knock on it three times," said Rab. "If you're cured it will open for you."

Donald knocked three times, and waited, trembling, hoping the gate would open.

*Creak! Creak! Creak!* Slowly the gate opened little by little, until there was room for Donald to pass through. As he walked through, *whizz-z-z!* Off flew the plate, down dropped the potato and meat, and away ran the kitten! The last

remains of the chocolate down his neck
and the sticky treacle disappeared, and
there was Donald, quite free from all the
things that he had carried about for days!

"Hurray!" shouted Donald, jumping
about with joy. "Do take me home, please,
Rab, will you? I'm quite cured now,
truly!"

"You wouldn't have found the Courteous Gate if you hadn't done someone a good turn," chuckled Rab. "So I know you must be cured. Come on! Jump into the plane, and I'll land you in your back garden in no time!" Off they went, up in the air, and down again slowly, and, *bump*! the plane came to rest.

"It's my own garden! Oh, thank you, Rab!" cried Donald. "Now I must go and tell Mummy all about it!"

He rushed off to find his mother, and oh, how glad she was to see him. She could hardly believe he had really been to the Land of P's and Q's, but when she found that he was always polite and kind, and never forgot a "please" or a "thank you," she knew what he said was true.

But I'm rather glad that when I sometimes forget to say 'thank you' for a cake, it doesn't jump off the plate at me, aren't you?

# Go Away, Bee!

Teddy was much too fond of sweet things. He knew where the jam was kept, on a low shelf in the kitchen cupboard, and at night, when he thought the toys weren't looking, he would creep downstairs, climb up on the shelf, sit beside the jam pot, and dip his paws in.

He always knew if the children had left any sweets about, too, and it did shock the toys to see him helping himself.

"They're not yours," said the big doll. "You know they're not."

"Some of them are now," said Teddy, patting his fat little tummy. "Ooh, they're nice. Have some?"

"Of course not," said all the toys.

"One of these days you'll be sorry," said the toy soldier.

"I shan't," said Teddy, and took another sweet. "I am never sorry. What's the use?"

"We shan't speak to you!" said the big doll.

"Good," said Teddy. "I always think you toys talk too much. If you don't speak to me or come near me I shall be very glad. You only frown and scold and nag."

"He's hopeless," said the toy soldier, walking off with the others. "A very nasty person."

Now, the next day the children had bread and honey for tea, and they were very pleased. Teddy stared at the honeypot, at the teaspoon that ladled the yellow honey out, and at the bread and butter so thickly spread with the lovely, sweet, golden stuff.

"Honey! I've never tasted it in my life! I really must try some tonight. If only the children's mother puts the honey on a low shelf in the cupboard!"

When she heard him say that the big doll frowned at him. "I know what you're up to, you naughty teddy bear. You're not to touch the honey."

Teddy waited till the toys were playing hide-and-seek. Then he went to hide, too – but he crept downstairs, of course, and hid in the cupboard where the honey had been left next to the jam. And didn't he have a fine time!

The toys went down and found him there, fast asleep, when they had finished playing. He was leaning up against the honeypot. They pulled him away.

"Look at his back! All covered with honey that has dropped down the jar!"

165

said the big doll, in disgust. "What are we going to do with him?"

"Leave me alone," said Teddy sleepily. "You're always stopping me from having fun. Leave me alone."

"You need a good bath," said the toy soldier. "Your back is all sticky with honey. We'll hold you under the tap."

"No, you won't," said Teddy, in alarm. "If you do I'll go to the brick-box and throw every single brick at you. And you know what a good shot I am."

"Oh, leave him," said the big doll, in disgust. "Let him be sticky if he wants to." So they left him, and went back to the playroom. Teddy got up, shook himself awake, and went upstairs to the corner where he usually slept for the night.

It was a fine, sunny day the next day. The children took their toys into the garden. They took the big doll, the teddy, the toy soldier, the pink dog and the black horse. They sat them all down on the grass.

Bees buzzed in the flowers all around.

Soon one of them smelled the honey on Teddy's back. It flew up and landed on Teddy's fur.

"Ooh! Ow!" squealed Teddy in fright. "A bee is walking on me! Chase him off, Toy Soldier!"

"Why should I?" asked the toy soldier, with a grin. "He's as fond of honey as you are. He only wants a little off your back, where you're sticky. Let him have it."

"You took honey when you wanted it. Why shouldn't the bee?" said the big doll.

"Quite right," said the pink dog.

"Go away, Bee!" yelled Teddy, and tried to flick the bee off his back. But he was too fat and couldn't reach right round. The bee stuck fast.

"It might sting me!" wailed Teddy. "Oh, take the bee off, somebody!"

But nobody did. They just sat round giggling and enjoying the fun. Ha, ha! Somebody else wanted honey and was getting it.

"Go away, Bee!" squealed Teddy, and wriggled his shoulders. "You're tickling me."

The bee flew off, but it came back at once. Teddy got up, turned his back to the fern growing nearby, and rubbed himself against the fronds. The bee flew away.

"Aha! You're off!" cried Teddy. "Now I'm going to lie down flat on the ground – then you can't suck at the honey on my back."

He lay down flat. The bee flew down and tried to crawl underneath.

"Mind it doesn't sting you!" called the toy soldier.

The bee managed to creep right under Teddy, and then the poor bear had to sit up because the bee tickled him so.

"GO AWAY, BEE!" he roared. But the bee took absolutely no notice at all.

"He's probably a deaf bee," said the big doll. "How awful, Teddy, you'll have to put up with him till every bit of honey is sucked off your back."

"I'll go to the pond and try to wash the honey off," groaned Teddy. So, with the bee flying round his head, he made his way to the pond. But he couldn't

reach to his back to splash the water there – and suddenly he lost his balance and fell right into the water!

The big doll ran to rescue him. "Whatever will the children say when they see you?" she said to Teddy. "You're soaked."

"They'll hang you up on the clothesline, pegged by your ears," said the toy soldier. The bear gave a scream.

"Oh no! Dry me quickly, big doll. Oh, here's that bee again. Go AWAY, Bee!"

The bee settled on Teddy's nose. The bear smacked at it with his wet paw. The bee at once stung Teddy on the nose, and he fell into the pond again, yelling loudly. The bee flew away, scared.

"Poor Teddy," said the big doll, and pulled him out of the water again. "I'd say he's been punished enough. We must dry him before the children come back."

So they dried him. Then he sat down in the sun to get warm. There was no honey on his back now, because it had all been wiped off in the drying.

"I'll never steal again," said Teddy solemnly. Then he suddenly looked scared. "What's this great big thing in front of my eyes?" he asked.

"It's your nose," said the toy soldier, and giggled. "The bee stung it and it's all swollen up. You do look funny!"

He did, poor bear. The children couldn't imagine what was the matter with him, and nobody liked to tell them.

# You Help Me, and
# I'll Help You

Jimbo was a beautiful Siamese cat. His coat was brown and cream, his paws were brown, and so were his ears and his face. But his eyes were as blue as the summer sky.

He had a lovely big garden to play in, but he loved to wander in the fields and the woods nearby. He liked to lie in wait for the rabbits, though he never managed to catch even a baby one, because they were all much too quick for him.

"It's really annoying, the way they all pop down holes as soon as I begin to chase them," said Jimbo, with a loud miaow. "I wonder if I could get down a rabbit-hole?"

Well, he tried one day, but a little way down he came to a big rabbit. The rabbit

glared at him, turned himself round at once, and kicked out at Jimbo with his strong hind legs.

*Biff! Biff!* Poor Jimbo got such a bang on the nose that he shot halfway up the hole. He scrabbled out of it very quickly indeed.

"I shan't go down a rabbit-hole again," he thought, washing his nose very gently with his paw. "My goodness! That rabbit went off like a cannon. BIFF!"

Now one day as he was wandering through the wood, he scrambled through a bramble bush. Some of the thorns caught in his fur and tried to hold him.

But he made his way through and came safely out of the prickly bush.

He ran on a few steps and then stopped. What was this pulling at him, scraping along the ground after him? He turned to see.

A dead bramble twig had caught hold of his fur and had held on round one leg. It was prickly and it hurt him. Jimbo sat down and tried to scrape the bramble spray off his back leg.

But it wouldn't move! All that happened was that the prickles pricked him harder. Jimbo mewed and ran on again, but it was no good, the bramble scraped behind him all the way and frightened him.

He fled up a tree, and the bramble went with him. He rushed down and the bramble rushed down, too. Wherever he went the prickly bramble twig held on tightly to him, and drove its prickles into his leg whenever he moved.

Jimbo sat down and howled.

"Ow-ee-ow-ee-OW! Ow-ee-ow-ee-ow-ee-OW!"

"Whatever is the matter?" said a small voice nearby. "Do be quiet! You'll wake my baby!"

Jimbo stopped howling and looked round. He saw a very small pixie peering out of a hole in the bank. The hole was neatly covered by a pretty curtain of moss, and she was holding back the curtain and peering out.

Jimbo stared in surprise. It was the very first time he had ever seen a pixie. Sometimes he had heard little pattering feet in the wood, and little high voices, but the pixies were very clever at disappearing as soon as he came near. Now here was one, with two tiny, pointed ears like a mouse, and two little eyes as green as the mossy curtain.

"You're sweet," said Jimbo. "Who are you?"

"I'm Tiptoe," said the pixie. "I live in this hole with Tiptap, my pixie husband. And we've got Tippy, the dearest little pixie baby you ever saw. You nearly woke him up with your dreadful yowls. What is the matter?"

"I'm sorry," said Jimbo. "But something has got hold of me and it's hurting me. Look!"

"Well! Whatever next? That's only a prickly bramble spray," said Tiptoe, coming out of her little home. "I can easily take that off for you!"

"Be careful you don't prick yourself," said Jimbo. "Ow! When you pulled, it hurt me! I got pricked!"

"Don't be such a silly," said Tiptoe. "You can't be much more than a kitten if you make a fuss like that."

"I'm not much more than a kitten," said Jimbo. "Oooh! Do be careful!"

"I can't pull carefully – the bramble is holding on too hard for that," said Tiptoe. "Now – just this last prickly bit and it will be all off!"

"Ooooh," said Jimbo. "That hurt, too. Is it really gone? Oh, thank you! I'm sorry I nearly woke your baby. Can I see him?"

"Well – I'll hold this mossy curtain up and you can peep in if you like," said Tiptoe. "But you're far too big for even your whiskery face to go in. Just peep, that's all!"

So Jimbo peeped into the hole behind the curtain of moss. The dearest little home was there – a long low room in the ground, hung with mossy curtains inside, and with a carpet of orange moss on the floor. Tiny furniture was there, made of twigs and leaves – and in a cradle slept the smallest creature Jimbo had ever seen – Tippy, the pixie's baby.

"I wish you could come in and have tea, but you can't," said Tiptoe. "Goodbye, now."

"Tiptoe, perhaps I can do something for you, one day," said Jimbo. "You've helped me – and I'd love to help you."

Tiptoe laughed. "You won't be able to help me," she said. "Pixies don't ask cats for help. Do go, because you really will wake Tippy. Look – here is a tiny ball for you. Tippy has so many he'd love to give you one. You can play with it."

She threw the tiny ball out of the hole and Jimbo bounded after it. It was hardly as big as a cherry, and just as red. He picked it up in his mouth proudly. He would keep it to remember Tippy by!

He hid it in his basket. Sometimes he sniffed at it and thought of Tiptoe and her kindness. He was afraid to go and see her again in case he woke the baby.

And then one night, when he was fast asleep in his basket on the veranda, someone came tugging at his fine whiskers. "Wake up, Jimbo, do wake up. Quick, Jimbo, WAKE UP!"

Jimbo woke up. The somebody pulled his whiskers again, and he mewed. "Don't. Who is it?"

"It's me, Tiptoe! Jimbo, you once said you'd help me if you could. Well, will you?"

"Oh, Tiptoe! Is it really you?" cried Jimbo. "And what's that you're holding? Your baby? What's happened?"

Tiptoe began to cry. "Jimbo, it's the rat – the horrible, nasty, big brown rat! He came sniffing into our hole under the mossy curtain, and he turned me out, and Tiptap, my husband, out and the baby out too. All our lovely furniture is outside the hole as well. The rat says he wants the hole to live in. Oh, Jimbo!"

"Well! The very idea!" said Jimbo, angrily. "How dare a rat do something like that? I never heard of such a thing!"

"What can we do?" wailed Tiptoe. "The baby was so frightened. And now I've nowhere to go tonight."

"Get into my basket," said Jimbo. "It's nice and warm. I'll go and find that rat myself."

"But, Jimbo – have you ever caught a rat?" asked Tiptoe, settling down in the basket with the baby and cuddling up against Jimbo's warm fur. "Rats are fierce. They bite sharply. They hang on to you and won't let go."

"I've never caught a rat," said Jimbo. "I've caught mice, though. And I'll go after that rat even if he flies at me and bites me hard. I won't have rats behaving like that to pixies like you! Now, you stay here in the warm and I'll go after that rat!"

He left Tiptoe and padded away to the woods. It was dark, but Jimbo didn't mind. He could see very well indeed in

the dark. He came to the bank where the pixie had her home. A small voice called to him.

"Are you Jimbo? I'm Tiptap, Tiptoe's husband. That rat is still in our home – and, oh dear, look at all our lovely furniture scattered everywhere!"

"How can I get the rat out of his hole?" asked Jimbo.

"Well, a squeaking mouse would bring him out," said Tiptap. "But no mouse will go near that hole tonight! The rat feasts on mice. So shall I tell you what I'll do?"

"What?" asked Jimbo.

"I'll squeak like a mouse – like a baby mouse," said Tiptap. "That will wake up the rat and bring him out in a rush. Then you must pounce. But be careful – rats are strong and fierce and afraid of nothing."

"Squeak away!" said Jimbo, hiding behind a big stone.

And Tiptap squeaked, "Eeeee! Eeeee! Eeeee!" It was a little high squeak that sounded exactly like a baby mouse's.

The rat awoke. He stirred in his hole. Tiptap squeaked again, a little nearer the hole.

The rat pricked up his ears. He sidled to the entrance of the hole. He saw a movement outside, and he pounced! The pixie fled under a stone, still squeaking. The rat had now come right out of the hole.

And then Jimbo pounced! But the rat heard him and fled, his long tail flying straight out behind him.

Jimbo raced after him, crashing through the bracken and the heather. This way and that the rat turned, and

then ran down a hole too small for Jimbo
to follow after.

Jimbo put his face right up to the hole.

"If you dare to go near Tiptoe's hole
again I'll catch you!" he cried. "I'm here!
I'll always be around, watching for you!
One day you will be my dinner. So make
sure you keep away!"

The rat shook and shivered and made
no sound at all! He could smell cat, he

184

could almost feel claws on him. Never again would he turn a pixie out of a hole.

Jimbo went back to the hole and called Tiptap.

"I didn't catch him, but he's gone," he said. "I don't think he'll come again."

"We'll have to spray it with bluebell perfume to get the rat smell out of it," said Tiptap. "You are very kind, Jimbo. Let me ride on your back, please. I'm very tired."

So Tiptap climbed up on Jimbo's back, and rode all the way to the veranda, bumping up and down as he went. He rather enjoyed it. Tiptoe and Tippy the baby were fast asleep in Jimbo's basket. Tiptap crept in beside them. Then Jimbo put in first one paw, then another, and then the rest of his body. He lowered himself down carefully.

Soon he was asleep too, the three pixies cuddled into his fur. When Jimbo awoke, they were gone! They had all gone home to the hole in the bank to see if they could put their furniture back, and hang up their curtains again. The rat had spoiled the carpet of moss, so they had to get another.

When Jimbo went to see them later that day they were settled comfortably in their little home again, and they gave him a wonderful welcome.

"What a pity you're too big to come and stay with us," said Tiptoe. "The baby does like you so much."

"Well, perhaps if you and Tiptap go away for a holiday, you'd let me have the baby to take care of," said Jimbo. "He could sleep in my basket, and I'd give him rides on my back. We could have such fun at night when I go hunting."

And, now I come to think of it it must be Tippy's little feet I sometimes hear pattering at night, down on the veranda below my bedroom! Because, as you know, Jimbo is my cat.

# The Mouse
# and the Snail

All summer long the fieldmouse had lived in his tiny little hole at the bottom of the sunny wall, and the snail had lived nearby.

At first they had taken no notice of one another at all, and then the mouse had began to wonder why the snail always took his house with him wherever he went.

"Why don't you leave your shelly house behind when you go out?" he said. "It seems silly to have to drag it along with you all the time."

"It may seem silly to you, but it's perfectly sensible to me," said the snail. "I have a very soft body, and unless I wear my house over it, birds might fly down and peck me up at once. You see, I

can't run away nearly as quickly as you can. I am a slow creature."

"Is your house heavy?" asked the mouse. "Can I come inside and have a look around?"

"Of course not. It just fits me," said the snail. "And no, it isn't a bit heavy."

"Shall we have a game?" asked the mouse, who was young and frisky and loved playing games. "Let's play hide-and-seek. You shut your eyes and I'll hide."

The snail rolled in his bigger pair of horns. "I'm hiding my eyes now!" he said. "My eyes are at the top of this pair of horns. I can pull them inside whenever I want to. Run and hide somewhere, little mouse."

The mouse thought they were strange eyes to have, but he was even more surprised to see the peculiar tongue that his new friend had. It was like a ribbon tongue, and it was set with thousands and thousands of tiny backward pointing teeth!

"Now you can see how it is that I manage to eat a whole lettuce leaf in a night!" said the snail. "I use my tongue exactly like a file!"

The two became friends, though the mouse never liked going for walks with the snail, because he was so very slow in dragging his body along.

Sometimes he left a bright silvery trail, and the mouse thought that was pretty.

"I shall have to say goodbye to you now," said the snail, one autumn day. "I feel sleepy, and I shall sleep for the whole winter."

"No, don't," said the mouse. "I stay

awake throughout all of the winter and I shall want you to play with me. If you go to sleep I shall come and wake you up. I shall knock on your shell or I shall tickle you to make you wake up!"

But when he next went to play with his friend he couldn't wake him up at all! How could he tickle the snail's soft body? The snail had grown a hard little front door over the entrance to his shell, and the mouse couldn't reach it!

"He's not asleep! He's dead!" wept the mouse. "And he was so nice. He won't answer when I knock on his shell!"

But he wasn't dead, you know. He was only asleep. He will wake up and play with the mouse again in the warm springtime. He may be in your garden, so hunt for him and see his hard little front door!